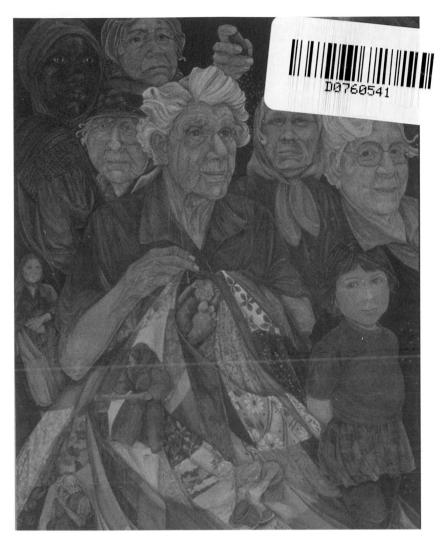

And My Name Is...
Stories from the Quilt

Margie Carmichael
Illustrations by Dale McNevin

The Acorn Press
Charlottetown
2006

And My Name Is... Stories from the Quilt
Text © 2006 by Margie Carmichael
Illustrations © 2006 by Dale McNevin
ISBN 1-894838-22-X

Editing by Jane Ledwell
Design by Matthew MacKay
Printing by Hignell Book Printing
Author photo by John Sylvester

We acknowledge the financial support of the Government of Canada through
the Book Publishing Industry Development Program (BPIDP) for our publishing
activities. We also acknowledge the support of the Canada Council for the Arts
which last year invested $20.0 million in writing and publishing throughout
Canada.

 Canada Council **Conseil des Arts**
for the Arts du Canada

The author would like to acknowledge and thank the Prince Edward Island Council
of the Arts for financial support while writing the manuscript.

 The Prince Edward Island Council of the Arts
Conseil des Arts de Île-du-Prince-Édouard

Library and Archives Canada Cataloguing in Publication

Carmichael, Margie

 And my name is— : stories from the quilt / Margie Carmichael ; Dale McNevin,
illustrator.
ISBN 1-894838-22-X

 1. Women—Fiction. I. McNevin, Dale, 1945– II. Title.

PS8605.A74A73 2006   C813'.6   C2006-904277-2

P.O. Box 22024
Charlottetown, PE C1A 9J2

www.acornpresscanada.com

To my sister Noreen and my brother Urban—
my best friends growing up
—*Margie Carmichael*

For Gloria Annette Doucette
"Her children praise her, and with great pride her
husband says, 'There are many good women, but
you are the best.'" (Proverbs 31)
—*Dale McNevin*

Contents

a.k.a. Angelica Rose

With the dawn
I arose to do my work
In this life

So much time has passed
Since I've begun
Yet my heart lost not a beat
In the rhythm of living
Even through the dark days
When my spirit was hunted down
To be made prisoner
Even in my own body

Yet my spirit lived
And journeyed through my eyes
Past the pain
To thrive in the realm of dream

In all this time
I am not gone
I am still here
With my songs of
Power and loss
Sorrow and gain
Biting down hard
Upon a changing wind
That carries my voice
Over walls and wells

Even if my teeth are gone
I will open my mouth
And sing of all I know

In cold comfort
I will enter my darkness
On my journey to my light
And another toothless face
Will pick up the song
As she travels through her darkness
To the cold comfort of her light

I am still here
And my name is...

Anna

In this hospital almost everything is white. I am not.

I was in my grove, talking to the trees. I should have been left where I fell. The leaves would have covered me. Mother Earth would have welcomed my body back. Instead, I was lifted from her embrace and carried away by flashing lights and wailing noise that drowned out the silence I was expecting. If our shaman were alive he would not allow it. He would turn away the white lights, white coats, and white masks trying to save the life of an old red woman who did not want to be saved.

As it was, they shot lightning through my body. From above I watched it jump, and it pulled me back in. My heart betrayed me and began to beat again. I cannot speak or move much of this body now. Most of it is dead to me. Only my foot has a life of its own. I think it wants to dance.

Be still, Foot. The Teacher Nurse is here.

"Class, this is Anna John. She is seventy-seven years old. Anna had a heart attack two weeks ago and a stroke six days ago. The right side of her body is still paralyzed, but she is stable. We are doing our best to keep her comfortable and free of pain. It was kind of her to let us visit. Are you up for it, Anna? Watch the left foot. Up and down means yes. Side to side would have meant no. Janice, touch that left foot gently now. How does it feel?"

"Really warm."

Foot feels the fear in her hand.

"Now, touch the right one."

My right foot feels nothing.

"It's ice cold."

"Can anyone explain the difference?" the nurse asks.

"The stroke has altered the blood flow on her right side?" a timid voice suggests.

"I think it's the wool sock myself," says the only male.

"Think about it on our way to Pediatrics," the nurse says. "Thank you, Anna. Do you want me to leave the lights on?"

Say no, Foot.

"Would you like the door closed?"

Say yes, Foot… We are leaving soon. The Other door opens wider now. Can you see it, Foot? The light coming through that door? It is a pure and gentle light—do you think it's Jesus?

…Bleep. Tick. Drip. Hum. Buzz. Click. The sounds in my room say I live still. It isn't fair! I tell you, Foot, it never was fair, in white world or red.

When I was taken from my family in my tenth summer I did not know I would never come back. Our reserve was remote and small, but they found us, Foot, and made us go to school. My brother Charlie, one summer older than me, made up stories all the time, and that summer before the school took us, he made up more stories to get us excited about leaving. In those days, we called him Laughing Dog.

When we waved goodbye with the other children who were going, Charlie held my hand. He was smiling, but I knew he was afraid, too. I could feel it.

At the school, Charlie and I were separated. Boys went with the Brothers; girls went with the Sisters. I didn't see him for two days and, when I did, I thought someone had died. His long dark braid was gone, and his face was swollen from tears and the shame that came with them. "They cut off my hair and burned it." He spat the words out and walked away from me. I screamed and ran after him, straight into the arms of the Superior. She locked me in a closet that night.

Next morning, my hair was hacked off. But I couldn't let them burn it, Foot! I grabbed as much of it as I could and stuffed it in my pockets, my shoes, my mouth. I was beaten, and my clothes were torn off and burned. They made me wear an itchy black dress, but they could not make me open my mouth.

I was locked in the church that night. My mother said church was God's tepee, but there was no fire, there were no cooking smells. The cold air was heavy with incense and beeswax. The only light came from a red candle that burned on the altar below the cross. I was told to kneel on the floor in front of the altar and beg forgiveness for my sins. The door shut and I was alone.

I looked up then and saw Jesus on the cross. He must have been very cold up there. He didn't have much on. Mother told me Jesus was born without sin, but they killed him anyway because people wouldn't stop sinning.

Foot, he was white, but the blood on his body was red, like the blood seeping out of my mouth. I don't know what my sin was, but I knew Jesus was suffering with me, locked in his own tepee. I made friends with him that night. I was afraid, but I climbed up on the altar, took the wet bloody hair out of my mouth, and hid it behind the sign on his cross. I promised Jesus I would come back for it.

Foot! The good nurse is coming. She is the only one who knocks.

"Hello. Anna. I need a little more blood from you. Can you make a fist for me today? I'll help you... I'm sorry, dear. I know it hurts."

My body doesn't want to give up my blood.

"Your veins are so tiny... Here's one. Atta girl!"

Foot, don't kick her. Save it for the Mean One.

"There! Almost done. I just have to take your pulse."

I won't be needing it much longer. The Other door is wider now. I see the light. I hear the whispers.

"Rest now, Anna." The nurse softly moves a strand of hair from Anna's eyes. "Rest those beautiful eyes."

Foot, the nurse reminds me a little of my Thomas, my husband. His touch was gentle and full of kindness. His was the first touch that didn't hurt me after I left my people. I had almost forgotten kindness.

I tried so hard to pretend I wasn't Indian... it didn't work.

Our parents died in a fire during my third winter of school. It stormed for four days, and Charlie and I didn't get to the funeral. One night we sneaked out of our rooms. Charlie lit a fire in the woods close by. We rubbed our faces with the ashes, cut off our hair, and cut our arms. We danced around the fire, drops of blood falling together on the pure white snow.

The Brothers soon discovered us. They knocked Charlie to the ground. He did not move. I thought he was dead, but I could not stop dancing. I wanted to die... dancing.

Faithful Foot, even when they broke two of your bones, you would not stop. You were so brave! Your pain kept me sane when they put me in the crazy house. Charlie lived, and he came to see me there. We cried for a long time. This time nobody stopped us.

After the tenth grade, I quit school to start a job Charlie found for me at a woollen mill making blankets for the troops in Europe. But before I left school, I kept the promise I had made to Jesus. The night before I left I went back to the church for my hair, and I let Jesus out of his tepee with a fire to warm his cold, uncovered body.

Later, Charlie said that it was him, that he had burned the church down. He was in jail for five years, atoning for my sin.

Foot, I know Jesus forgave us. He said a lot of things about children— it's in the Bible... let the little children come to me... to such as these does my kingdom belong... heaven help the one who harms a hair upon the head of one of these.

I visited Charlie at the halfway house after he got out of jail. We were in our twenties then. I was still working, and Charlie was drinking heavily. He was broken, but he was mending. His hair was long again, and even when he was raving drunk, he sometimes spoke in Mi'kmaq. I didn't know what he was saying—the language had been beaten out of me a long time ago.

It was at the halfway house I met Thomas. He was Métis from northern Saskatchewan. His father was French and his mother was Cree. We married in 1949 on the Feast Day of Saint Anne, my namesake. And didn't we dance, eh, Foot?

A month after our wedding I got a letter from Indian Affairs telling me I wasn't an Indian any more because I married a Non-Status. Why had they tried so hard to destroy us when it was so easily done on paper?

I got even more Indian after I married Thomas. He told me all the legends and stories of his people. They became my people. He meant to teach me Cree, but another war began. I didn't want him to go, but his father was in the last one, and Thomas left for Korea. A sniper killed him. They sent his body back to me. I will take his medicine pouch with me so he can find me in the next world.

He didn't know we had a daughter. Matilda was six months old when he died. In my grief, I cut our hair. I braided Matilda's with mine, then I cut myself. While I was in the crazy house again, my daughter was taken from me. I prayed she would look for me, so I could give her her braid. It's in the basket I made for her, and so is her father's medal.

Foot, I miss her! My tears are rivers in the valleys of my neck.

The Mean One is coming. I can smell her spirit. She's putting all the lights on... must be afraid of the dark.

"You wet yourself again! Why didn't you press the buzzer? You can use one hand, can't you?"

What a lazy Indian I am!

"Now I have to make your bed again!"

She has heavy feet. She must have an angry heart. There were always mean ones, Foot. I think bad spirits attach themselves to weak people, to make themselves feel strong.

"You're getting a diaper tonight, missus!"

I'd rather moss. Even thistles are kinder than you.

"I'm not allowed to take that filthy sock off, but I don't have to look at it! Under the blanket with you!"

Patience, Foot. She's leaving soon. She's angry at Charlie, not you. He took the Grand Chief in to see me yesterday. They prayed for guidance on my journey. The Mean One tried to have them thrown out for burning the sweetgrass and sacred tobacco, but the hospital would not dare stop the Grand Chief. He told them to sit me in a chair so I could greet my ancestors with dignity. He has a powerful spirit. I had nothing red to wear for my journey, so Charlie took off one of the red socks I made for him, and he put it on you, Foot. I thought she would blow up! She hates Charlie. She can always smell liquor on him. I can only smell campfire.

Just a little longer, Foot. We have to wait for Charlie. I hope he will live in my house after I'm gone. I miss my little house. After I got out of the crazy house, I got another letter from Indian Affairs, telling me I was Indian again because Thomas died. His death wasn't worth much to Canada, but I got enough money to buy a piece of land beside the new reserve where Charlie went to live. He really wanted me to live with him, but when I decided to live alone, he helped me build my house. It's his now. I hope he will find peace there, like I did.

Our Shaman helped me heal. I saw no more hospitals, till now. I have taken no man since Thomas, and I kept my body covered to honour his memory.

Look, Foot! Do you see them? Over there by the window—our people are waiting for us! They have drums and feathers. They are singing.

"Daughter... it is time."

Charlie is here! He is crying! Help him!

"You must say goodbye."

I cannot speak!

"Sing, daughter... sing... your spirit can sing."

"...nmultes njiknam—goodbye my brother..."

"...nmuknam nkwejij—goodbye my sister..."

Foot! Charlie is setting you free. Oh! Charlie, the Mean One is coming... She is pushing my brother away. Oops! She tripped.

Thank you, Foot... the Laughing Dog is laughing again.

Old Grey House

How many hands have touched your doors?
How many feet have walked your floors?
How many hearts are longing for this old grey house?

Old grey house down the road,
You have the saddest eyes that I've ever seen,
And the wild morning-glories grow
On your shaded face where you once were green.
Sepia pictures on your walls
Long-ago secrets in your halls
Are still as the autumn leaves that fall
'Round this old house.

Old grey house down the road,
You have the saddest eyes that I've ever seen,
And they're wide open to the winds
That can take you travelling to where they've been.
Tattered white curtains flap and fly,
Waving to summer friends gone by.
I cannot pass but I feel and cry
For this old house.

> I remember we were dancing on the lawn—
> We drank hot tea after midnight.
> We were staying up till dawn—
> There were stories by the firelight.
> Warm friends on a winter's night
> And swordfights with the icicles that clung
> To this old house.

Old grey house down the road,
You have the saddest eyes that I've ever seen.
Now they're boarded up and blind
To the life that was and what might have been.
Old apple trees root deep in sod,
Reaching their naked arms to God.
Forgotten fruit will bud one day
'Round this old house.

Tansie

Alice sipped her tea and waited for Tansie to sit down. She enjoyed their visits and had missed Tansie in the years that she was away. They grew up together and were never lost for something to talk about. Today, though, Alice had something on her mind and wasn't into the chitchat that usually went on while Tansie flitted around her kitchen—not that Tansie noticed, so absorbed was she in looking for the sugar bowl. "Now where did I put it this time?" she asked herself. This happened a lot. Tansie was absent-minded—always was.

"For God's sake, Tansie, never mind the sugar," Alice said as she poured Tansie's tea for her. "We're sweet enough."

Tansie flopped into her chair across the table from Alice. Sunshine slanted through the windows and lit up Tansie's distracted face. "The crabapples will soon be ready."

"Speaking of crabs, Evelyn called me last night. She was worried when you didn't answer the phone."

"My niece is a worrywart." Tansie blew on her tea. "Caller ID is a great invention."

"Ignoring her will only make things worse. She's not the type to be put off." Alice shook her head. "She called me twice this week."

"She's after me to move to town for the winter."

"She's worried about you being alone here, that's all."

"But I won't be alone." Tansie leaned toward Alice, her eyes sparkling. "I rented out the other side of the house. My tenant is moving in the first of next month."

Tansie was at the kitchen table reading the paper when the car drove up the lane. Evelyn stormed in the kitchen door. "Just what do you think you're doing?"

"What are you talking about, dear?" Tansie asked innocently.

"What's this about you taking in a boarder?"

"Actually, I'm renting to a tenant."

"Aunt Tansie, how could you!"

"It was easy. I put an ad in the paper."

"Why didn't you return my calls? I had a line on a lovely apartment, down the street from my office." Evelyn turned her back to Tansie and crossed her arms severely.

"Makes more sense for me to get rent than to fork money over to someone in town." Tansie was cool as a cucumber.

"I can't believe you—"

"I know you mean well, Evelyn." Tansie put the paper down to wait for the inevitable tirade.

"You're seventy-two years old! You live twenty miles from town—a mile from your nearest neighbour." She was pacing by now. "Your lane is a quarter-mile long, the power was out four days last winter—"

"And all I got was a cold."

"It could have been pneumonia! What if you fell or something?" Tansie shook her head and sighed. Evelyn wasn't going to stop. "Or a seizure?"

"I haven't had one in years."

"What if you'd run out of medication?"

"I'd have to get more, wouldn't I?"

"What if you couldn't? It's not like an aspirin, Auntie—you have epilepsy. Did you tell your new tenant that?"

"Sit down, Evelyn, you're making me dizzy," Tansie chuckled.

"It's not funny," Evelyn sighed. She plunked herself down beside Tansie, took her hands, and looked into her dancing eyes. "You drive me crazy... you really do." Evelyn got up to pour some tea. "So, tell me about this tenant. Who is she? What does she do?"

"His name is Ubie, U-B-I-E. He's a night watchman at the meat-packing plant in town."

Evelyn dropped her teacup before it reached her lips.

"Evelyn's not too pleased with you renting to a man," Alice declared over a fresh hot biscuit.

"She'll get used to it."

"She'll be bothering you more now, you know. I don't think she'll like him."

"Doesn't matter. I like him. More tea?"

"Just a half a cup. What's he like?"

"Quiet, hardly says a word. Keeps to himself."

"Does he have family?"

"Didn't ask."

"Friends?"

"Don't know."

"Then what do you know about him, Tansie?"

"He's in his early fifties. He took all his things here in one half-ton truck load. He'll help with the wood, and he doesn't want a phone."

"Does he drive a black truck with plywood sides?"

Tansie nodded.

"Is he a big, big man with hardly any hair?"

Tansie nodded again.

"Well, I'll be! That must have been him at the gas station. He had a big roll of page wire in the truck. Haven't seen page wire in years."

"He's putting up a fence around his side so he can park his truck there."

"He has his work cut out for him, then, if he tries to tame your wild kingdom back there, Tansie. Must be a lot of work to look after it." She looked out the window to Tansie's garden, a riot of blooms and grasses, with flowering weeds holding their own beside more deliberately planted flowers.

"Mother nature does the work," Tansie said. "I just putter. And play." Tansie had mischief written all over her face.

"If I didn't know you better, Tansie, I'd think you were senile."

Tansie raised her teacup and touched Alice's. "If I am, I have to admit that my second childhood's a lot more fun than my first."

Tansie was in her backyard pruning roses. The October sun was warm on her face, and birdsong filled her ears. A big grey cat lay on a flat stone beside the fence, sleeping off his morning meal. Tansie was still amazed at how her cat had adapted to the loss of his hind leg last summer. Thank heavens the driver stopped in after hitting him. Most wouldn't. The young woman felt terrible and helped Tansie look for him. Somehow, he had managed to drag himself back up to the yard. They found him hiding in the hawthorn hedge, trying to bite off the crushed leg. The first thing he did when he came home from the veterinary hospital was to drag himself down to the basement to use his litterbox. With the funny looking e-collar around his neck, he looked like a drunken bride. If only humans could accept our losses like that, Tansie mused.

Her cat was named Methusaleh, and Tansie hoped he would live a long time. He was oblivious to birds now, though he would still catch rats, mice, and occasionally toads, which he formally offered to Tansie, intact and unharmed. He still didn't understand why she let them go; sometimes he was actually offended.

Tansie was happy today. Ubie was bringing a pet home. She knew it wouldn't be a cat, as Ubie wasn't fond of them, though he was starting to get used to Methusaleh. She'd hardly seen Ubie in the month since he'd moved in. He worked nights and stayed inside most of the day. He was so timid yesterday when he asked her about having a pet. To a man who didn't see much sun or many people, she would never think of saying no. She only hoped it wouldn't be a big dog.

The new fence Ubie had put in extended from halfway through the backyard, over to the hawthorns, and along the row until it crossed again to end at a gate attached to the front side of the house. It was crudely built but would hold a dog. It wouldn't, however, keep Methusaleh out, Tansie considered. Lost in these thoughts, Tansie didn't hear a car drive up.

"So there you are!" It was Evelyn. "I need to talk to you. Can we go inside?"

Tansie sighed and took off her gardening gloves. "All right." She could tell from Evelyn's voice that it would not be an easy visit—or a long one, if Tansie had anything to do with it.

Their last visit hadn't gone well. Evelyn had met Ubie, and "didn't like the look of him." "What kind of a name is that?" she'd asked him, none too kindly. Ubie's face had turned beet red, and he'd looked away. Tansie had glared at her niece, but her voice was almost musical. "It's short for Hubert, isn't it Ubie?" He was halfway out the door already. Evelyn's words had hung in the air like frost.

Once inside, Tansie didn't offer tea. No use pretending all was well. "So, what do you want to talk about?" She poured herself a glass of water and leaned back against the countertop.

"Aunt Tansie, I'm sorry about what happened with Ubie."

"It's him you should apologize to, not me."

"Please! Just listen." She sat at the table. "There's something you should know about Ubie. I did some asking around."

"How dare you!"

"It's for your own good, Auntie."

"Like hell it is!"

"He was in Riverside for four years."

"He had a nervous breakdown."

"You knew, and you let him stay?"

"Your father let me stay."

"That was different. Nobody knew you had epilepsy."

"Your grandfather knew, a year after he put me there. I was twelve years old."

"What?"

"He never told my mother. She died believing I was possessed by the devil, or something foolish like that."

"Oh my God!" Evelyn was truly shocked.

"He took me to her funeral then sent me back to Riverside for another five years! If it wasn't for your father I'd still be there. Six years altogether. Am I crazy, then?"

"No! My God, no. I'm sorry... I had no idea."

"Well, now you do, so don't go judging a person when you don't know the whole story."

Ubie liked living in the country. It was quiet, and he had more privacy than he'd had in a long time. Tansie was a very nice landlady. She minded her own business and didn't even ask for references. He was a little leery of her at first, as he wasn't used to people who smiled so much. In Ubie's experience, such people were highly medicated, drunk, or up to something.

At first he'd agonized over telling her about Riverside. She'd find out sooner or later, he thought: the Island is a small place. Better she refuse him right off the bat than evict him later. Tansie didn't even blink an eye, though she did ask him about medication. "Well then," she said. "I'll remind you to take yours if you remind me to take mine. I have epilepsy. Deal?" They shook on it.

Tansie was the first person in years to invite him to dinner. He bought new pants and a shirt for the occasion. Ubie wasn't much of a talker, but Tansie more than took up the slack. She told him all about the house: how it was designated a Century Farm Home in the late 1970s; how her brother Bob (Evelyn's father) renovated after their father died and made a place for her beside his family (Ubie's place now). When Bob and his wife Jean had retired to Florida two years ago, she moved to their side of the house. The house was hers now, and she let the back gardens have their way. "Bob used to mow it all to within an inch of its life," Tansie chuckled. "When he was here last summer he painted a sign: 'Welcome to Mutual of Omaha's Wild Kingdom. No admission, but you may never find your way out.' I'd have left it up, only he used watercolours! He worked on it for hours out there with the blackflies, and him bald as a baby's arse. The rain wiped it out in two minutes! God, we laughed!"

She told him all about Methusaleh and his accident. From his seat beside Tansie, the cat hung on her every word. He had his own place setting. As well-mannered as Methusaleh seemed to be, Ubie still wasn't sure about him, especially now that Ubie had so many pets.

The first one he brought home was a blind budgie that had been returned to the pet store. Next came a young crow with a broken wing. Ubie found it limping along the highway. Tansie was so relieved he wasn't bringing home dogs, she gave him the go-ahead. It wasn't long before he had quite a collection, all of them birds, most of them abandoned or broken in some way. For the first time in his life, Ubie had a family to care for, a secure home, and a real friend.

Tansie and Ubie had had only one run-in so far, shortly after he moved in. He was mowing his yard, and she saw him cut down some wild roses that wandered through the fence and onto his side. She was very upset with him. "Turn that damn mower off!" He'd never heard her swear. She was shaking and in tears. "I can understand you chasing my cat, but no one has the right to condemn a rose if it wants to grow! Push them back through the fence if you don't want them!"

He didn't see her for three days, and he didn't sleep a wink. She knocked on his door one morning. Ubie opened it, expecting an eviction notice. She quickly closed the door behind her, mindful of the birds. There she was with her smile, and an eyeful of tears trying not to fall on the plate of fresh-baked biscuits she handed Ubie. The birds interrupted any apology she might have uttered. Chirping, squawking, flying, they introduced themselves to Tansie, who laughed and clapped her hands in delight. Ubie was shaking so much, a biscuit fell off the plate, to be claimed by the crow. One look at Ubie and

Tansie mercifully left to "rescue her next batch from the fires of hell." Closing the door behind her, Ubie softly cried his eyes out and, with great relief, fell asleep at last.

⚯

By mid-December Ubie had colour in his cheeks from being out-doors, shovelling snow, chopping wood for the furnace they shared. One day he was carrying an armload of wood and Tansie threw a snowball at him, knocking his cap off. He was mildly annoyed. Then she threw another, missing him this time. He set the wood down, picked up a fistful of snow, and threw it at her. Soon they were into a full-fledged snowball fight, ducking behind trees, chasing each other around the house and the hedges. Tansie laughed her head off. Ubie took it a little more strategically, though he was careful not to pack the snowballs hard. Tansie won. After they caught their breath, they made a snowman. Ubie picked his cap out of the snow and put it on the snowman's head. Tansie let out a whoop. "Oh my God, he's a twin to my brother, Bob!" They doubled over laughing and knocked the snowman down in the process. Bob fell apart. They were hysterical.

Tansie invited Ubie over for a Christmas Eve supper with Alice and Evelyn. He was relieved that he was scheduled to work. He had successfully avoided Evelyn very well so far, though he knew Tansie was playing peacemaker. Maybe next year, he told her. "That's only two weeks away," Tansie mused. He wasn't off the hook yet.

⚯

The drive home on Christmas Day took longer than usual. High winds and blowing snow made his weary eyes work harder to see the road. By the time Ubie parked the truck he could hardly see his tire tracks. A surprise waited on his doorstep. A red ribbon, tied around the middle of a fifty-pound bag of birdseed, blew in the wind. Beside the bag was a huge clear plastic Christmas stocking with Ubie's name on it, filled with chocolate bars, dried fruit, jars of cranberry jelly, and a new woollen winter hat with earflaps. From Santa. He almost cried. He dashed to Tansie's door to wish her Merry Christmas, knocked twice, but there was no answer. She must've gone to church with Alice. He hoped they had stayed put, and that they weren't on the roads trying to get home.

He knew something was wrong before his key turned in the lock. The birdsong was frantic. Ubie walked into total chaos. Sparrows and jays dived and rose, afraid to land. The pigeon was on the mantelpiece, bobbing her head in muted coos. The budgie was in the only cage, but even with the door open, she clung to the perch while the cage swung back and forth from the ceiling. The crow was strutting around the floor like a sergeant-major. "Calm! Calm!" he seemed to say.

Ubie softly whistled and the fliers came to him, all anxious to tell him what had happened. He stroked under their necks, one by one, until they quieted down. At his feet, the broken ones gathered, their little hearts beating like triphammers until Ubie stroked them, too. The cage finally stopped swinging. He counted: the birds were all there. He wondered what had spooked them. The storm? By now it was a blizzard.

Feathers, birdseed, and droppings covered the floor and furniture. He went for the broom and noticed the basement door open. He was sure he'd closed it after loading the furnace last night. He felt a draught. The fire was out. Tansie must have forgotten to load it this morning. He was about to put the broom back when he saw red clay footprints leading from the basement and into his hallway: unmistakable three-legged footprints. Methusaleh. He started down the stairs so fast, he tripped and fell most of the way, landing against bags of potatoes before he hit the floor and blacked out.

<hr>

When he came to, it was pitch-black, and Ubie didn't remember where he was. His grandfather's voice shouted from every corner of his mind: "Get up, you lazy little bastard!" Ubie waited for the boot. "Ugly!" Crack went his ribs. He couldn't move. "Bastard!" Whoosh went the switch across his face. His grandfather's spit landed, mixing with the blood. Another kick. "Clean yourself up!" His grandfather staggered away.

There were rumours of a young child at the bootlegger's, but few saw him, and their credibility was dubious. Once the rumours proved true, the authorities of the day made the grandfather send the boy to school. By then he was nearly eight years old.

"Name?" asked the teacher on the boy's first day of school.

"Ugly bastard," he replied, trembling. Slap!

Nobody bothered to ask the bootlegger why his grandson didn't have a proper name. At the school he was called Ubie. It was another year before the authorities intervened.

"He's my whore-of-a-daughter's bastard," the grandfather told the welfare worker. "Ran away with her slut of a mother, came back long enough to drop him in the back bedroom, then she took off again and left her bastard here for me to rear!"

"What is his given name?" the worker almost spat the words, barely able to control her rage, one hand trying to do the paperwork, the other trying to soothe the frightened little boy who clung to her skirt.

"Let me spell it out for you, Missie," the old man grabbed the papers out of her hand. "'U' for Ugly. 'B' for Bastard. That's what he is." He threw them at her. "Now get him out of my sight before I kill the two o'ye!"

Grandfather's words echoed in Ubie's mind as he lay on the basement floor, until they faded back into dull memory. He still couldn't move. Something heavy landed on his chest and gently licked the tears that ran from his eyes. Methuselah. And Ubie remembered where he was. From a far corner of his mind he heard a call for help. It was Tansie. The cat went flying as Ubie hauled himself up, only to fall down in pain when a leg went out from under him. He crawled across the basement floor to Tansie's stairs. The cat was already at the top. "If you can do it, Methusaleh, I can do it," he panted, and started up the stairs, dragging his leg behind him.

"Help me... Ubie, help me," Tansie called out. He found her lying on the kitchen floor, shivering in her nightgown. He took his coat off and put it over her. Tansie was very weak. "Thank God you found him, Methusaleh. Good boy!" she held her cat close. "Oh, Ubie! I was taking my meds, and I tripped over a chair and spilt the whole bottle, but I got one into me. My head is awful sore."

"I'll call 911. Try not to move," Ubie said. He crawled over to the phone, made the call, and gave the particulars. He managed to pull himself up to the sink and get a glass of water for Tansie, though he spilled half of it on the way back to her.

"Ubie, you're hurt!"

"I'm all right. Don't you worry about me. The ambulance will be here as soon as they can get a plough through. Tansie, you have to stay awake, understand? It won't be long."

"Too cold to sleep."

Ubie held her hand. "Merry Christmas, Tansie."

"Merry Christmas, Ubie! Did Santa come?"

He kissed her forehead. "Yes, she did."

It was another two hours before the ambulance came. Ubie and Tansie talked the whole time, about his years in the many foster homes, her life with a stern and loveless father, their years in Riverside. They agreed that the wrong people were locked up. They cried for each other and laughed with each other. They were still laughing when the ambulance arrived. Ubie held her hand all the way to the hospital.

Alice drove Ubie home the next afternoon. He was lucky: no broken bones, but a badly sprained ankle that would keep him home for six weeks. Tansie had a concussion and would be in hospital long enough for them to give her a thorough check-up.

That evening, Ubie heard a knock at the door and hobbled over to open it. Evelyn stood there. "I just wanted to thank you for taking such good care of Aunt Tansie. If you hadn't been here..." She wiped her eyes. "We got off on the wrong foot, you and I... I'm sorry." She gave him a teary smile that reminded him of Tansie. "Can we start over?"

Ubie reached for her hand. "My name is Hubert. Would you like to come in?"

Brogan's Quest

Upon the Hill of Tara where dwelt the Celtic kings,
Before unseeing mortal eyes there be a magic Ring.
But Brogan, being a bloodson from the noble tribe of Dan,
Could see the princess daughter dance, and sought her fairy hand.

When Finn, the roguish leprechaun did see young Brogan bold,
He chuckled to himself, "Oh Finn, now here's a pot of gold!"
He whispered then to Brogan, "If the dream be yours to win,
You must steal the Silver Pillow from the Ancient Fairy King."

Now Brogan, being enamoured in the magic of the dawn,
Should have been suspicious of the dancing leprechaun.
But his wiles and wits had vanished, like the dew before the sun,
And a fire burned inside a heart that knew what must be done.

In the full moon of Midsummer's Night the fairy folk rejoiced,
And the wisdom from a timeless age rang in the old King's voice.
He sang of deeds and things to come, still waiting in the stars.
With a gentle hush, he stilled the winds, and silence took the guard.

But Brogan stepped within the ring; he took the Pillow from the mound.
Thunder raged across the sky, they trembled at the sound,
And Brogan's spell being broken, in wonderment he stared
As Finn took the Silver Pillow, disappearing in the air.

"The magic you have tampered with, young mortal," said the King,
"Cannot be tamed by humankind or kept within this ring.
Now it's loosened to the madness of a worldly leprechaun,
And a curse I put upon you for the wrong that you have done."

"Brogan, you will never sleep...
Brogan you will never die . . .
Brogan, you'll not see our kind again—
Until you find that rascal Finn and bring the Pillow home again
To the hill of Tara and the Fairy King."

While Brogan wept, the oldest race vanished from his sight,
And the laughter of the leprechaun echoed in the night . . .

The raven's wing, like an icy wind, gives shiver to the spine,
And Brogan's quest is ended if faith passes from our minds.
But in these times of dreams lost, like shadows at our heels,
There're Brogans to pursue the dream and Finns the dream to steal.

Buttercup

It was the coldest winter anyone would remember, and the tiny Island of Gairn was completely cut off from the Irish mainland town. The harvest was abundant in comparison to other years: the animals were fat from summer grazing, dried fish hung on strings from ceilings of rooms facing north, there was plenty of wood, and all musicians and storytellers were home and accounted for. There were few babes that year, human or animal, and with no elders abed, the 107 hardy islanders felt little cause for concern. The last thing they expected that winter was a new arrival.

They say she blew in with the north wind—for lack of any other explanation, since all the boats from Gairn or the mainland were frozen solid in ice until the spring. Jack (the Jackal) Doyle was the first to spy her and was out of breath by the time he arrived at the alehouse with the news that morning.

The Jackal had a nose for news, and when there wasn't any, he made it up. No one minded him much nor liked him—for he was more a liar than a storyteller—so when he first blurted out his story the men did not immediately abandon their mugs of ale to crowd around him and offer him a mug. He was quite upset.

"I saw her, I tell you! Ran uphill against that wind with a pack on her back, and her feet never touched the ground—I swear on my good wife's grave, God rest her soul!"

Alban, steward of the alehouse, handed the Jackal a mug. "Sure 'twas likely Maigret's ghost you saw, still running away from you. Sit down!" This time the men turned around, and laughed, for everyone knew that Maigret ran off with a mainlander not long after she married Jackal, who insisted she'd drowned and was eaten by the fish. Jack wasn't any woman's cup of tea, even in the best of his days, for he was not a clean man in word or manner. Now he was past his prime, bitter, balding, nearly toothless. When he wasn't talking or drinking, his tongue hung out of one side of his mouth and he drooled from the other—hence the name.

"Ye won't be laughin' long, lads! It's the tinker's ghost that's come, and she'll ruin every last one of ye!" Jack turned his stool to the stove and his back to the men. Last night's ale and spittle pooled on the floor. For a moment, the sun came in a window and shone like silver on the wetness, while the wind howled high and mighty, drowning out the laughter of the men.

It was that evening that everyone discovered there might be some truth to what the Jackal had said. Alban was opening a fresh barrel when he looked out the window and suddenly yelled, "Fire! Fire! Logan's Wood's on fire!" Thirty-some men grabbed their gear and headed for the door. In less than fifteen minutes, all available buckets on the island were filled at the well, and a procession of islanders was carrying them up the hill to Logan's Wood. Women, men, and able-bodied youth trudged through the snow with the sun setting behind them and the fire rising in front of them. At the well, older men harnessed impatient horses while barrels of water were loaded onto a feeble old sleigh. The conversation was almost festive.

"Might have to make a few trips."

"Been a while since we've had a fire."

"Big enough to be the house."

"Better the house than the woods."

"Could burn down the whole island with this wind!"

"Shut yer gob, O'Leary!"

It was slow going, but the sleigh made it up and over the hill. The horses dearly wanted to turn away from the smoke and flames, but persistent hands steered them forward. Rounding a corner onto the woods trail, horses, men, and sleigh stopped dead in their tracks. Ahead, a line of islanders stood around a circle, still as stone, buckets in hand and mouths agape.

In the centre, a huge bonfire shot up into the night sky from a long-forgotten fence tangled up in itself, old wood sighing and cracking at the touch of the flames. The Logan house was lit up, but with the tame fires of candles in every window. From the front door a little woman clapped her hands in delight. "Do you like what I've done to the place?" she asked. The bewildered collective nodded as one, trying to remember the house that—until this night—was falling in on itself and slowly being swallowed by the surrounding woods.

That night the house looked like it had in its grand years when the old Master Logan was in his prime. Though he owned the island by law, he was a generous landlord and a good man, too—good to his tenants, and fair. Twice a year all the islanders were invited to the house to celebrate, in April at the departure of a bitter winter, and in October after the crops were in and the sheep were shorn.

Widowed young, he had two sons. Paddy was the eldest, and not at all like his father. He hated any kind of work and resented that the tenants didn't treat him like the little lord he thought he was. None of the boys would put up with him, for he was mean and spiteful. It might have come from growing up without a mother, but he was no better with the girls.

The younger son, Sean, was another story altogether. Something happened to him in the the woods one day when he was a youngster and he was never the same. He couldn't talk after that, but he was nice enough, all right. He grew into a big strong lad and was given to wandering, showing up at anyone's house anytime and scaring the wits out of the old women, even if he showed up just to do them a good turn. Ah, but he was harmless, and kind like his father. Despite the size of him, he was one of the best dancers going and a favourite with the older girls, especially if they didn't want be bothered by some of the older boys who came over from the mainland.

For all that he was mute, his eyes and smile spoke of a gentle soul who found joy in the simplest of things. Anyone who took the time to observe Sean examining the workings of an ant colony or following a bee among the wildflowers would be as helpless as he to find words that could describe the delighted wonder and mystery on his face. The only one who didn't take an interest in or a liking to Sean was his brother, and when Sean was having a good time, Paddy was miserable. Poor old Logan couldn't do a thing with him.

Things took a terrible turn when old Logan died. It was a bad winter, and like many of the older ones, he couldn't fight the fevers that wouldn't let go. Paddy took right over, gave his father a half-arsed wake, and that's the last time the islanders darkened the door of that house. Poor Sean dug the grave all by himself and wouldn't let anyone near him to lend a hand. It was a pitiful sight, this big hulk of a young man gouging out the frozen stony ground, working up a sweat that mixed with tears and turned to ice that coated his chest and surely broke his big beautiful heart.

No one saw much of either brother for a few weeks—and that

was to be expected—until one morning out comes Paddy with the old Master's horse and riding cart. Sean was trussed up in the back of the cart, bruised and bleeding from the back of the head. Paddy rode slowly past the people who came out to watch, looking each one in the eye till all the eyes looked down at the ground. He took his brother off the island across the ice and left him in the asylum on the mainland. There was no celebration that April.

While the other islanders stood gawking at the bonfire at the Logan house that night, the Jackal was not among them. He crouched in the woods and watched in disbelief as the spellbound islanders followed the woman into the house. There was music for the longest time, sweet music that called Jackal to join the others, but he knew better. The sky had cleared and when the full moon shone down from the centre of the sky, the doors opened. One by one the silent islanders walked back to their homes, leaving the sleigh and all the horses behind.

There was no sign of the woman after they left. The fire slowly died in the snow, and the candlelight left the windows. Shortly after, the sky clouded over and hid the moon. Jackal rose on stiff legs, thinking it time to move, now that he could. He fought the urge to run like hell, for he knew it always made things worse, the imagination usually getting ahead of a fellow that way. In the blink of an eye she appeared in front of him.

"So, Jack Doyle, you're not the fool they think you are." Her form shimmered, shifting from the tiny cringing woman so familiar to his memory to a dazzling beauty of a woman, regal and tall, whiter than light. "Which of us frightens you most? Me?" asked the regal woman, "Or Buttercup?" She became the tiny woman once again. Jackal nearly fainted for, sure enough, no one but Jack had called Paddy Logan's tinker wife by the name of Buttercup.

He was shivering now, but not from the cold. As her form shimmered again, he could not take his eyes away from the light. "Come with me, Jack Doyle." A terrified Jack Doyle followed her into the house, afraid beyond help. When the door closed behind him, he had a feeling he'd never be the same, and he was right, for when he drank the warm nectar she put to his lips, he fell deeply asleep and dreamed of Buttercup.

The Jackal was absent from the intrigue the following morning, as in twos and threes the islanders tried to figure out if what had happened at the Logan house was real or if they'd all had the same dream. It was a long time since anything this exciting had happened on Gairn, and they didn't quite know what to make of it. The talk was cautious, though, for there were secrets threatening to whisper. It was all a little strange to those islanders who hadn't been there that night, a lot of whom attributed the stories to too much ale after the fire.

Imagine! The Logan house back to itself and herself throwing a party! Now, that was rich!

"Show me the house then," one of the women challenged her man. Like many others, he wasn't willing to go back. "You're full of blarney. Get out of my way and do something useful—like find the horse!" Naturally, he went to the alehouse, for if it was the tinker's ghost, and it looked like her all right, there might be an accounting.

Paddy Logan was a hard and bitter man. In a matter of weeks after his father's death, the peace and contentment the islanders had known with the elder Logan were but a dream. Paddy went to every house and announced new laws. There were to be no more trips to the mainland without his consent; he ordered all debts settled by the end of that year's harvest, or the tenant faced eviction; a quarter of all fish caught was to be his in exchange for the use of his boats; thievery would be punished publicly; there was no more access to his woods; tenants were to purchase peat from Paddy's bogs on the mainland; music, stories, and merriment were forbidden. By the time winter came, the island had lost twelve families who could not pay their debt, and by spring the rest were low on food, fuel, and joy.

A year after Paddy took Sean away to the asylum, he went to the mainland again. When he came back a week later, he brought back Sean, and a woman.

Sean was greatly changed since the islanders last had seen him. Gone was the innocence from his face. In its place was hardness. The eyes, that once danced as he did, were empty and stared straight ahead. The huge hands, that had so gently cradled so many of the newly born, hung limply by his sides and did not move to protect him from the jostling of the wagon on the stone-covered road. There were tears from many eyes as they saw what had become of him, tears that fell on their feet once their eyes met Paddy's.

The woman sat between the brothers, small and darker than any woman on the island. Her clothes were patched, her hair was long and matted, and her hands were tied in front of her. As she passed, she held every eye. Poor though she looked, her bearing was straight and proud. Defiance roared under the silence. As the islanders watched the wagon make its way down the road, many prayed for protection, and as many offered thanks that, for the time being at least, Paddy would have no need for their daughters.

That summer, Paddy had Sean build a sturdy high fence around the house. Some of the younger children who Sean used to coddle and entertain came by to watch, but Sean chased them away. They ran home frightened and confused and were told to stay away from Sean.

The woman was seen only when she came to the well with Sean. By now, it was known that she was a tinker, given to Paddy in exchange for a spring foal and an iron pot. Any compassion or kindness offered to her was met by a cold stare from her and a warning glare from Sean, leaving the islanders in an offended state that permitted indifference to Paddy's doings. She filled her pails with water, and as she walked away, her skin, dark as it was, could not hide the darker bruises on her legs and arms. In the winter, heavier clothes hid them well and made it easier for the islanders to pretend they were not there.

For Jack Doyle, there was no pretending. As keeper of the ledgers for the tenants, he spent many hours at the Logan house. Paddy chose him for several reasons. Jack had a head for numbers, and Paddy did not. Jack was also already not liked by many of the islanders because of his loose tongue, and Paddy learned a lot from that tongue for the sake of a few pints of ale here and there.

Since Jack's wife had run away years before, he missed the contentment of a home with a woman's spirit. In Paddy's home, though, there was no contentment. The spirit of Paddy's woman was like that of a captured bird, and in the beginning she tried to get away at every opportunity. After a time, when she settled down a bit, she reminded him more and more of a buttercup, battered by storm and wind, fragile and yearning for the sun—a tough little buttercup that kept on growing just for spite, rooted in the stony ground that was her life with Paddy Logan. He admired her for that, but he feared for her, too.

Jack never witnessed anything, but he knew that Paddy beat her. Everyone else knew too, though it was easier to blame it on Sean, since it was Sean who meted out punishments to anyone caught doing anything Paddy thought of as thieving. It wasn't Sean, though, who had scratches on his face or who bled from his nose when she fought back, and it wasn't Sean who locked himself in his room at night with a bolt on the outside of the door. It was Paddy with the fists and the locks, both. Neither Sean nor Paddy needed the doctor from the mainland from time to time.

That next spring, there came a day when things went too far. Jack came to the house unannounced, with the full intention of telling Paddy he was leaving Gairn. Jack could no longer bear the islanders' resentment, and with more than a few stolen pints in him, he was about to tell Paddy he was taking the woman he thought of as Buttercup with him. He strode in without a knock and saw Paddy on the floor, eyes wide open, a look of surprise on his dead face. The woman was bleeding on the floor by Sean's door, barely alive. The door was hanging on one hinge. There was no sign of Sean.

He carried the woman down the road and knocked on every door asking for help, but none came. He took her to Paddy's boat and rowed over to the mainland. The doctor took one look at her and shook his head. That was the last he saw of her.

It was the face of Buttercup that Jack saw when he opened his heavy eyes in the morning after drinking the nectar. "So, Jack Doyle, do you still think me a ghost?" she asked. Jack rubbed his nearly naked head. "I don't know what to think—but whatever you gave me to drink last night was better than the best ale I've ever had, and I'd thank you for another—if you please." For the first time, he heard her laugh, and he almost felt like dancing. "Once you've tasted the nectar, there's no going back, but there'll be no more for you just yet, Jack Doyle. Get up now, and we'll have a bit of a chat. I'm sure you're loaded with questions."

Paddy sat up and came right to the matter. "What are ye then if yer not a ghost?"

"A faerie, though not a high-ranking one, for all that I'm the

King's daughter. This woman you call Buttercup is not real," she said while changing form, taking on her former height and beauty, "but I am."

Paddy looked at her a long time before he spoke. "The old people used to tell stories of what they called a 'glamour.' Was that what she was?"

"Yes, a glamour she was. It was my father made me the tinker woman, to come back and undo a mistake I made when I came here once before—a mistake that robbed a child of the life he was meant to have. Do you remember when Sean Logan was just a little boy? When he was found after being missing in the woods?" Jack nodded and sat up a little straighter.

"I was in those woods, hiding as I often did from my father, the King of all Faeries. I had strict command to remain unseen to mortals. I couldn't resist the child asleep so peacefully on the leaves, so I took him with me, just for a while, and we travelled through the planes together. Time belongs to us in the world of faerie, and time passes differently on your plane—but I learned too late that mortals are not meant to journey as we do. I took Sean back, but the damage was done."

Tears came to Jack's eyes, remembering this special lad and thinking of the tormented man he had become. "And for that, you ended up with the likes of Paddy Logan." The faerie looked away.

"He was a regular visitor to the tinkers' camps on the mainland. The one my father sent me to was only too willing to get rid of the strange woman who had joined their caravan one night. My powers were fettered within the glamour, and I couldn't stop Paddy from taking me away. I didn't recognize Sean when Paddy took him from that horrible place, but what Paddy did to him here was unbearably worse, and I couldn't help him. My father intended to teach me a lesson. That he did. True enough."

Jack said nothing, taking it all in and nodding his head as it all began to make incredible sense. The wheels began to turn in the mind of the man who had forgotten and reinvented the larger part of his life.

"You've always had the sight, Jack Doyle, but you did not get the chance to explore or understand it. The King of Faerie himself knows not where it came from, nor what to do about it except keep a distance from this plane. There aren't many of you left now, people with the sight, and strange as it may seem to you, the faerie world needs you and your dreams to continue to exist in ours."

"I don't understand."

"Nor do we. There is a higher being at work, that even faeries cannot comprehend, despite our magic." Tears came to her eyes and ran like silver rain to her quivering lips.

"I didn't know a faerie could cry."

"We're more alike than either of us know."

"What became of Sean?" The question was abrupt, but it was a fair one, and necessary at this point, for the day was getting on.

"Since the day of Paddy's death he has been with my father, safe and mending. Nearby."

"The mainland doctor said Paddy died from fright. Was that your doing?"

"No, or I would have done it sooner. Paddy was at me worse than ever before, and Sean was pounding on his locked door. My father heard me calling and came at last, in all his raging glory. The sight of him took the living breath from Paddy, and when Sean broke through the door he couldn't bear what he saw. He fell to the floor, and held us both in his arms, the lost child that he always was. When you came to help me, my father vanished, taking Sean with him. If my mortal body had died, my spirit would have vanished for eternity."

This was a lot for Jack to absorb, and he was grateful when he was sent to deliver a very important message to the islanders.

⸙

At the alehouse, more people than usual were gathered in the afternoon. The horses had not returned, and the cold wind had been blowing for hours. Most were content to stay right where they were.

"They'll not come home with this weather on," said one man.

"They'll be all right till the mornin'," said Alban, not wanting to lose the patrons.

"Good shelter in the woods," said O'Leary.

"Looks like you chickens need some grit," said a disgusted woman, trying to get her man to go home.

When the Jackal came in, the talk dropped on the floor with the spittle. It suddenly occurred to them all that they hadn't seen him since last afternoon. There was something very different about the Jackal, but they had no time to figure out what it was, for he left as soon as he delivered his message: "Every man, woman, and child is to come to the Logan house at sunset. There will be food and drink for all."

The men drank up and went home to their families.

The faerie and Jack were watching from the woods as the procession made its way up to the house. The sun was setting as the full moon was rising. The sky was clear, and the bonfire burned anew.

"There will be many not pleased to have a master again," said Jack.

"They'll get over it," she said.

"How will he explain the house?"

"In time, they'll nearly all believe the tinkers had something to do with it. They're blamed for nearly everything, anyway."

"Usually for thieving, though. This will baffle them here for generations."

The islanders were not expecting to see Sean Logan waiting for them, especially those who were in no hurry to have him back. He was older now and looked much like his father had. There was something in his stance that was unfamiliar, a calmness that belied the years under his brother's domination. He stood beside a small bonfire, its light showing the magnificent life that leaped from once-empty eyes.

There was no enchantment upon them now, and the islanders' whispers echoed back and forth among them like a breeze in the trees—until Sean began to speak, and they were shocked into silence as still as the fresh-fallen snow.

"I've been away a long time, and for most of my life I've been a stranger to myself—but I remember everything that happened here. In these flames are the tallies kept by Paddy Logan and Jack Doyle. We can begin again. I ask forgiveness of anyone I've harmed, and I ask you to forgive my brother, who was lost as much as I was, in a different way. Please come in. Welcome to my home."

As the doors closed, the faerie's eyes looked deeply into Jack's.

"Are you sure this is what you want?"

"More than anything."

"Someday you will die as all mortals do."

"I don't mind dyin'. It's the livin' that's hard."

"True enough."

"Since we're to be travellin' companions, should I call you M'Lady, Yer Highness, or what?"

"Buttercup will do."

"Any more of that nectar around?"

"Not yet. You're not ready."

"That's disappointing."

"You will be more disappointed when you meet the leprechauns."

"Can't be any worse than the mainlanders."

At that she laughed as fully as she ever had, and, like tiny bells, her laughter rang in the air and came to the ear of Sean Logan who, tending to his guests, learned again to smile.

Only the intended ear heard the whisper that followed: "Come away, Jack Doyle, with me. The best is yet to be."

Calling Johnny Home

The heron spread its wings up to the sky
And loosed a cry across the water.
The mountains took the echo to the Great Lakes
And the golden fields.
Through the window of a home that's not his home
An old man hears
And the memory of a salt-water sunset
Shines in his tears.

O Johnny, can't you hear
The Island voices calling you home?
Your travelling is done —
Oh, hear the Island calling you home.
Prairie breezes caught you flying,
In your youth you had to go —
Now your aging soul is crying for
The peace the silent harbours know.

O Johnny, can't you smell
The sod a-turning underneath the plow?
The snow is on your brow,
You must be tired,
Won't you please come home?
For your heart lies in the valley
And your soul roams the seashore.
Won't you come back to your Island,
For your work is done forever more?

Irini

When I was young, my favourite hiding place was under Grand-mother's burqa. It was a place of shadow, full of secrets. Grand-mother did not mind me there, even if she was wearing it, as long as I was quiet and didn't ask questions, like, "Where is the rest of your foot? Do the stripes on your back hurt?" It was a place of mystery and imagination: my desert tent. The scent of cloth, the scent of spices I would trade for shining gems, and her scent, the scent of home, surrounded me. There, I always felt safe.

In our part of the world, Afghanistan, sons are gifts, while daughters are less so. When Ahmad was born, my world became smaller. I didn't know, with my five-year-old eyes, that the tiny help-less creature devouring my parents' attention might someday have the power and the right to determine my future.

My father was a surgeon, and we lived in a three-bedroom house on the outskirts of Kabul. We were not wealthy, but our living was good. Mother kept a garden and sold her produce in the market. I loved being with her there. She was different than when she was at home quietly fussing over Ahmad and praying I would grow up soon and marry a nice man who would be good to me. At the market, she turned into a proud, shrewd merchant who haggled and bartered well and laughed about it as we walked home with the other wom-en.

She was beautiful, my mother. She always loved colour, her light cottons and silks dancing around her when she moved. When a rare, cool breeze came in summer, she hung her clothes outside, and at night when she took something in to wear, it was as if she took the breeze in with her. She was quiet when my father was home in the evening. He would read to her from the Qu'ran, first the prayers then the poetry, which she memorized and recited to my brother and me before we went to sleep.

My brother Ahmad was always a pleasant boy, and we all adored him. During the day he was very active and loved being outside. He was curious about everything in his world. My mother was too busy and tired to keep up with him, so it was my job to keep him occupied.

In the evenings after our father came home, he became the serious son and followed our father like a shadow, listening, asking many questions, waiting for one embrace before sleep. It was I whom my father embraced, until Ahmad came along. I was jealous at first, until I learned to become invisible.

While Ahmad slept in the heat of the day, I practised being invisible under Grandmother's burqa, and I learned to be silent and still. It was the only place Ahmad would not enter to find me when he awoke. Perhaps it was the darkness, but he seemed afraid of the burqa and of Grandmother. I don't know why. All she did was sleep, pray, and cook—an arrangement that worked well with our mother, who thanked Allah for the rare gift of a mother-in-law who treated her like a daughter and did not interfere. Grandmother was also very good at being invisible.

When the time came, I was happy to go to school. My mother had not learned to read and did not want that for her daughter. At school, I missed the solitude I sometimes had at home, but I did not miss the demands of my little brother, who now slept in my room. By then I had become good at causing no trouble, being obedient. My mother would say, "You will be a good Muslim woman, Irini. We will find you a husband that deserves you."

Ahmad and Father prayed together every day. Their prayer mats were side by side, and on Ahmad's eighth birthday, they agreed they would make their pilgrimage to Mecca together.

"When will you take me to the mountains?" Ahmad asked Father.

"Someday," Father responded. "The mountains are not going anywhere."

"But what if we have to leave Afghanistan?"

"Then we will go through the mountains." Father remembered his own impatience as a boy and was patient with his son.

<hr>

When I had my first blood, I was frightened. I did not know what was happening to me. Mother told me that I was becoming a woman, that Allah was preparing me for having babies. After that, I had to leave my room with Ahmad and was made to sleep with Grandmother. My father spoke to me even less. "I do not want to be a woman! I do not want to have babies!" I told Grandmother. She wrapped her arms around me, kissed my face.

"The child will always live in the woman you will be," she said. In her rheumy eyes I saw something I'd never seen before, a brightness that seemed out of place with her wrinkled face.

Grandmother was still my safe place. She dried my tears and corrected me when I needed it. She taught me much about Islam, more than anyone else. In Grandmother, I saw the beauty and wisdom behind the ritual. She loved Allah and talked to him all the time, though my mother called it muttering.

While the eyes of the world were watching, the Russians came in 1980. Afghanistan was not prepared. We became prisoners in our own country, locked away from the rest of the globe. Our forces were disorganized, but resistance continued, especially in the mountain regions, the mujahideen nipping at the Russians' heels like wild dogs.

In those years, our family was more fortunate than most. Our part of the city was not as badly damaged by the bombs and artillery. My father was a skilled surgeon, valuable to the Russians, and was escorted daily to the hospitals throughout Kabul. Many nights he was taken from his sleep to where the rebel prisoners were kept, and he was forced to choose from among them who would be treated and who would be killed. He became an old man very quickly, and at home it was as if he wasn't really there.

Ahmad was becoming a young man and, like all of the young men, was angry and filled with frustration. He became hostile to our father, defiant and disrespectful. He no longer listened to the women of our family. He spent a lot of time with other boys, after curfew. Sometimes when he came home there was blood on his clothing. One night, Father caught him cleaning a rifle. He hit Ahmad so hard I thought it would break his neck. Ahmad knocked Father to the floor. "You are a coward! You do not see what they've done—to our children, our women!" Mother was shrieking, but Grandmother slapped her into silence. Violence hung in the air, a venomous snake striking at the heart of our family. Ahmad picked up the rifle, packed a sack, and left us that night to join the resistance. He was fourteen years old.

My mother was never the same after that night. She became silent and lost interest in living. She abandoned her garden, which had grown smaller every year for lack of seeds. I did my best with it and went to market in her place. There was little to see or trade, and our women no longer laughed.

Grandmother, on the other hand, came back to life. She mysteriously acquired packages of wool, mixed in texture and colour, and she spent much of her time knitting socks, which just as mysteriously disappeared on a regular basis. We knew Ahmad was still in Kabul. Father said to her once, "Socks will not stop bullets."

"No," she said, "but they warm the feet that run from them."

Though I missed Ahmad, I was glad to have my father back in my life. He relied on me more and more, as my mother was so broken. I could no longer be invisible. With all the damage to the city and the loss of life that came with it, there was a shortage of help at the hospitals. Father taught me from his medical books, and soon I was going with him as an assistant. The Russians in the hospitals were less frightening than those we met on the streets. They needed Father's skills and compliance, so they did not have him under guard. They did not see the small supplies that I took from the hospital and hid within my clothing, to leave our house in Grandmother's socks.

At the hospital, it was strange to look upon the young, suffering, helpless Russians as the enemy. So many just wanted to go home. We knew the resistance was succeeding because the Russian casualties were rising. International blockades prevented medical supplies and equipment from reaching the hospitals. I began to run out of things to steal.

When the Russians finally withdrew, they left behind a landscape littered with landmines and broken or abandoned tanks, planes, and weapons. They also left hundreds of soldiers unable to leave the hospitals. Soon, our hospitals overflowed with our own wounded, too. Father did his best to ensure that the Russian patients, now prisoners, were protected. There was a special section in our hospital for those severely damaged, who would never know or see home again. Father took a special interest in them, since they were so much like my mother, lost and with little hope.

With my father's blessing, I attended university in Kabul. He thought I would make an excellent nurse, but I intended to be a doctor. I loved my studies and was hungry to learn all I could. Never was life so precious as in those first few years of freedom after the Russian occupation, as Afghans tried to rebuild our country. I realized how safe I had been under Father's protection. Though I studied hard, my real education came in the clinics and shelters that sprang up in the city. I learned from the impoverished homeless, the victims of torture, the children maimed by landmines, and the many widows with children and no family left alive to take them in. I understood why my brother called this a holy war. What was done to our people was unholy.

My brother was right. But so was our father.

Late one summer evening Ahmad came home for the first time in three years. Even Father cried at the sight of him. Ahmad never lived at home again, and there was great tension between him and Father, but they did not speak of what had happened between them. Over the next few months some of Mother's spirit returned, and she spent time in her garden, bringing it back to life. Ahmad and I spoke mostly of the survivors we knew and their experiences, but he would not speak of his. He was very proud that I was in university but would not tell me his own plans. Grandmother kept to herself most of the time, but often Ahmad came to her window, and they talked quietly, late in the night. I listened sometimes, invisible again.

"You do not understand," she told Ahmad. "Your father did not grow up with war like you or me. He sees the cost every day at his hospital. It does not make sense to him. You must respect that."

Ahmad was troubled. "Afghanistan belongs to Afghans, not to the rest of the world, no matter how much they think to help us. I fear that war is coming again."

"War always comes," she said, "but we survive."

I doubt my brother envisioned the extent of the change that came. From the seeds of unrest, dormant during the Russian occupation, civil war grew in all its bloody glory. The victor that emerged was a dark, angry monster that consumed the spirit of many Afghans. The Taliban takeover was swift and ruthless, bloody and bitter, obsessed with purification. Islamic law, shari'a, which was given to protect and guide the spirit, became a weapon that, in the hands of the ignorant, turned Afghanistan against itself and the world. There was a higher power at play, but it was not Allah. Had I uttered such words at the time, I would have been executed.

I learned to survive as schools were shut down, institutions came under heavy guard, food became scarce, and fear seeped into every heart. It was far worse than the Russian occupation. The mullahs screamed the new laws from every mosque, to be heard beyond the cities and villages, in the smallest tents of the desert. For most Afghans, especially women, it was a step backward into hell.

Education was forbidden to females. Female bathhouses were shut down. Women were to wear the burqa at all times to conceal our bodies from all but close relatives. Make-up, high heels, shoes that made noises, nail polish, jewellery, movies, music, dancing, and videos were outlawed to prevent idolatry. Women were prevented from attending at hospitals; in the few exceptions, women had to wear a hijab to talk to doctors if they needed to discuss a patient. Drivers were not allowed to pick up women in burqas. No tailor could measure a woman for clothes. Prostitution, adultery, and homosexuality were punishable by death. Drug consumption was forbidden. These were some of the rules established by the Department of Promotion of Virtue and Prevention of Vice, enforced by the Religious Police.

This time I was not spared from knowing. There were executions and public punishments daily. People on the street were herded towards the public spectacles, forced to witness and participate. There were stonings of prostitutes and adultresses. Most of the men participating in the punishments were the same men who had seduced or raped the accused women in the first place and had then testified against them. Homosexuals were half-buried in sand beside ruined walls, and the walls were made to fall, to bury them alive. There were amputations for theft or dishonesty, whippings for the slightest offense. In front of me one day, a woman was given seven lashes because she had a bell on her bicycle. A young girl had her ear cut off because she wore an earring.

Ahmad urged Father to take us out of Kabul. Father spat in his face, "There is nowhere to go." Father would not allow our women to leave. Ahmad left Kabul, joining others in the mountains to fight the Taliban.

It was not safe for women on the streets. Mother refused to leave the house, refused to wear the burqa. Her fear drove her to madness again. One night Father did not come home. He was executed three days later. We were dragged from our home and forced to watch as his hands were chopped off. Then he was shot. His crime was trying to save the Russian prisoners from being murdered in their beds. Mother hanged herself that night in her garden. Grandmother never spoke to anyone again, but still prayed to Allah. She stopped taking food and drink, and one day her beautiful heart stopped beating. I buried her beside Mother and Father deep in the garden. I was alone.

For two years I survived the insanity, leaving home only at night,

Margie Carmichael — **69**

stealing food, hiding in the shadows. At home I sought sleep and mumbled to Allah, all hope gone from my heart. Grandmother's burqa could protect me from the terror I could not make invisible, but it could not shut out the sounds of despair. Fathers mourned daughters who took their lives; mothers keened for the sons taken to the madrassas to be educated in the Qu'ran, weapons training, and martyrdom. Babies cried for food that would never come. Some families were so desperate and afraid for their girls that they cut off their daughters' hair, disguised them as boys, and sent them away to the madrassas just so they would not starve to death. Once discovered, the girls did not survive.

Ahmad came back for me one night and took me out of Kabul. We hid in the mountains, making our way through the heavily patrolled Khyber Pass to the Pakistan border. During those weeks with my brother, my desire to live returned. In the camaraderie of the mujahideen safe camps, I saw the happy little boy that was my little brother. In his tender care and devotion to the wounded, I saw my father. He left me at a refugee camp, with American dollars sewn into the clothes under my burqa. It was the last I saw of him.

After two years in the camp, I was accepted into Canada and joined other refugees in Toronto. I live in a small apartment in a poor area of the city, but our community is rich in freedom and opportunity. I have three jobs and take classes to prepare for admission to medical school someday. I do not know if Ahmad survived to see the Taliban driven out, or if he ever got to Mecca. Someday I will go back to Afghanistan, if only to find his body and bury him in our garden, if it still exists. The Allah that I believe in will welcome us all into Paradise someday, with hot tea and fresh flowers.

I did not burn my burqa, my grandmother's burqa, like so many women did. It hangs in my closet, in darkness, alone among brightly coloured scarves and garments once forbidden. These other clothes keep a safe distance, afraid of its heavy stillness. Yet the burqa remains, a presence, a part of my story and my world.

Sometimes, when a cool breeze comes through my window in summer, I think of my mother. Clothes she would have loved so much to wear rustle and sparkle when I open the door, and I often wonder what they were discussing before I interrupted them. The silk scarf tells me nothing, always seeking a way to slip unnoticed from my head. It is not faithful, would go to any head, then slip away again with the slightest notion, and feel no pity for the pin or clasp left behind unable to explain.

Babies Are Born

Babies are born, somewhere among us
Just like in Bethlehem that night
Babies are born, just like in Bethlehem
Somewhere among us tonight

Some will be hungry, somewhere among us
Just like in Bethlehem that night
Some will be hungry, just like in Bethlehem
Somewhere among us tonight

Some will be lonely, somewhere among us
Just like in Bethlehem that night
Some will be lonely, just like in Bethlehem
Somewhere among us tonight

Some will be homeless, somewhere among us
Just like in Bethlehem that night
Some will be homeless, just like in Bethlehem
Somewhere among us tonight

Some will be exiles, somewhere among us
Just like in Bethlehem that night
Some will be exiles, just like in Bethlehem
Somewhere among us tonight

Mom and Tessie

She was stubborn and smart and made wonderful oatmeal cook-ies. She didn't want her grandchildren to call her any of the "old people" names, so we called her Tessie like our father John and his brothers and sisters did. Our mother, every bit as stubborn and smart as Tessie but more conscious of her status, called her "Mama Tessie" on a good day, and "that one" on a bad day.

If ever there was a troop with two generals, it was ours. Mom and Tessie were very different women, but by the time the last half of our brood was mobile, they had had over a decade and the older half of the ten children through which to establish that they were equally matched but well aware of pecking order.

No matter what we did to the one, or that we did it, we could run to the other and most times get away with it. When we didn't get away with it, we learned the power of a united front and the humili-ation of a disciplined rear.

Home was not really a war zone, but it looked like one some-times. With ten children living there over almost thirty years, it was chaotic at times, and most of all for us last few children. We were good, sweet children, but our combined energy ran from the theatric to the barbaric, and we youngest had come along when neither Mom nor Tessie had much get-up-and-go to get up and go chase after us.

We were an imaginative brood and often got carried away with our collective energy, so we were easily distracted and sometimes disobedient. At such times, neither Mom nor Tessie was very patient. Unsure as to which one of us did or didn't do "it"—whatever the "it" was—Mom would recite the litany of the daughters while Tessie threatened the boys with hell and hard labour. We rarely rebelled when it came to homework or catechism. Both the women valued education and instilled in us a sense of responsibility for ourselves in our various futures, something that went deeper than a desire to please them. When they were proud of us, they showed it, and we thrived on their praise.

Theirs was a baffling relationship. When they had words with each other, they cut deep. Their words were angry, loud, and spared no relatives or ancestors. We were frightened when they were mean to each other. We didn't know what to do to stop it. An older brother or sister usually took the lead, and we would follow to the loft or to the playhouse in the grove to seek the less complicated company of other children. If it was night, we'd go upstairs and try not to listen. We had no idea how bad it felt for them to feel the way they did in those arguments—not until we were older and had our own arguments. Families forgive incessantly.

Tessie's Scottish roots were as stubborn as Mom's Irish ones, and in the more harmless spats, when the two women merely jousted, Mom's final touch was to start singing "The Massacre at Glencoe," at which Tessie would salute the Black Watch and recite her lineage as far back as Rob Roy MacGregor, concluding with the words, "Put that in your pipe and smoke it!"

Five minutes after one left the room, the other would send one of us out to see if she wanted a cup of tea. The two of them would act as if nothing had happened—a tacit truce. Taking a break from the daily grind, they would listen to the radio news, giving their opinions on it, then would resume their day with sporadic chatting that encompassed family, neighbours, community events, and world events. In the event that any little ears were caught idly eavesdropping, they would assign any number of chores to get us the hell out of their kitchen.

Naturally, anything we overheard was repeated and exchanged with other little ears from other kitchens, at a game of ball across the road or in the nearest hayloft. (Just as naturally, some of those sessions were overheard by bigger ears). Every now and then some juicy tidbit made its way into the wrong kitchen and little ears were boxed—a natural response to bigger ears hearing something they didn't want to hear. It was easier for an adult to box ears than to confront the initial offender—usually another adult. We learned a lot about diplomacy; we also learned that adults were confusing.

Our father John, familiar with the ways of adults, did his best to not get caught between Mom and Tessie, knowing full well he'd get the worst of it if he did. There was no fooling or pacifying either of them, but he knew ways of keeping the peace: getting as far away as he could, making light of them, or writing a song about them on the spot. When there was music at the house, they all gathered around Mom's organ in the parlour, with our father on the mouth organ, mandolin, or guitar, and Tessie keeping time with her cane on the floor. We all performed in one way or another, mostly singing. Many times visitors would bring some "treats," and after a few shots Mom and Tessie would be singing each other's favourite songs together, though neither woman would ever admit she approved of liquor.

Tessie had still not forgiven our father and our Uncle Duncan for setting home brew and getting caught by the Mounties some years before. To top it all off, John had told the Mounties the barrel of brew belonged to Tessie. It took some strategic visits to the Premier and a ten-dollar fine before the incident blew over, and, just when it did, our father wrote a song called "Tessie's Can" and sang it all over the place. Mom knew every word.

Along with the songs came the stories, especially the ghost stories. From an open grate in the kitchen ceiling, we all had a turn at eavesdropping on conversations about forerunners, ghosts, and unnatural events. Though Mom and Tessie didn't tell so many stories, they backed up those who did, from time to time adding details.

The superstition in our Catholic home perhaps came from Scottish and Irish generational memory and tradition, but it was definitely reinforced by ritual and natural events. Death was close to home in those days. In our own house, our grandfather Dan had died at home and was waked in the parlour. He was also embalmed at home, and his blood was poured on a nearby field, where it fertilized the ghost story tradition as much as the soil.

Thunder and lightning provided more opportunity for superstition. When storms were happening, it was hard to get all the children inside the house. We wanted to see it, to feel it, to hear it. Chain lightning was the brightest, but, according to Tessie, fork lightning was the greater threat to our souls: "The Devil's doing his work!" We'd hide as long as we could, usually in the loft, counting the seconds between the thunder and the lightning, till it got so close we were scared and ran for the house. When we got to the house, we often wondered if we'd have been better off taking our chances with the lightning and staying put in the loft. Inside the house, Mom and Tessie would be on their knees and would immediately begin daubing us with holy water, handing us the beads to say the Rosary, the oldest ones taking turns at leading the Decades. Sometimes we got through all the Joyful, Sorrowful, and Glorious Mysteries, if the storm lasted long enough.

Joy, sorrow, and glory united these women through all their shared experience. Tessie helped Mom with all the babies, and both women knew the silent grief of miscarriage. Fortunately, neither had to go through the agony of losing any of the ones that survived to birth. They cried with each other when Mom's brothers left to fight in the Second World War, when Tessie's husband Dan died, when Mom's parents died, when JFK died, when Pope John XXIII died, when *Dr. Kildare* went off the air.

Our father John's health was an issue from the day he was born and throughout his life. His lungs were weak from bronchitis, asthma, pleurisy, pneumonia, and emphysema, so both women were used to carrying him out of the house or field or barn and rushing him to the hospital. Tessie stayed with us while Mom waited at the hospital. We'd be waiting to hear from her, quiet for a change, bargaining with God in our thoughts. The kitchen clock ticked, the fire crackled, and the rocker creaked as Tessie rocked the youngest, humming quietly some old air she didn't know the name of. The phone would finally ring, and we'd all hold our breath till Tessie said, "Thanks be to God!" We would say a Rosary in thanks to let loose all the pent-up energy; Tessie would only yell if we woke up the baby. When Mom got home, she and Tessie would go in the bedroom off the parlour and shut the door.

Both were farmwomen and worked hard with the animals and the crops. Tessie was good with the horses. She drove a mail route in her younger days and had a firm hand with a frisky young stallion. Mom preferred the older mares with their gentler temperaments, and from what we heard, they preferred her to Tessie, who wasn't very patient. They worked side by side in the fields and most of the time they talked, though our father would separate them sometimes if it was necessary or if his teasing made matters worse. Privacy was rare in that big family of ours, so we took advantage of their time in the back fields to wander over to the line fence for blueberries or to have a pee break in the windbreak.

In summer when friends and family came from away, Tessie was the reigning queen and Mom her begrudging lady-in-waiting. The older people had status and took full advantage. When Tessie's friends came from Boston, she sometimes went over the top trying to impress them. We'd all be made part of the mad dash to clean up the house. She and Mom would bake for days and hide everything, a lot of which we found and got into.

We weren't the only threat to the baking. One day, with company expected, we were absorbed in following the mothercat, to find where she had hidden her kittens. She led us to the old stove in the corner hallway and ran in behind it. When we lifted up the top of the stove, there was a pan of date squares under a dishtowel. And lying on the towel were three newborn kittens, which the mothercat promptly took away, one by one, to another hiding spot. When the company came, Tessie served the squares, which were all eaten before we got home from strawberry-picking. We never said a word.

Occasionally, Tessie would use the cover of her company to give Mom a little dig. She would whisper loudly when Mom left the room, "She's a poor housekeeper, that one!" Equal to it, Mom would yell back, "It's a poor house to keep!"

Still, Mom and Tessie relied on each other when anyone was sick or if there was a crisis. They shared the love and responsibility of our father and the children, sacrificing a good portion of their lives to keeping our home going. They often acted like martyrs to get their way, but as we grew older, we came to know that in the older generations, praise, gratitude, and attention were rarely given when needed or deserved. Such things might have made children "big-feeling" or "full of themselves." Many later died from humility.

Tessie lived a long life, most of it in good health. She could still pick potatoes on her hands and knees when she was ninety. Mom's health was more of a struggle, with heart problems that ran in the family and stress that came with raising a large family in changing times. Even so, when Tessie began to slow down, Mom looked after her at home. It was not easy on either of them, but they kept things down to a dull roar. In the fall of 1965, Tessie fell and broke her hip. She was in hospital for nearly eight weeks. It was a long time for us, but we knew she'd come back home, just like our father always did.

We all remember the day she came home, on Friday, October 29. We were anticipating Hallowe'en, which would fall on the Sunday that year, so we were going out trick-or-treating on the Saturday. Tessie came home in the ambulance, and there was quite a celebration. She sat up by the fire after supper and listened to us talking to her all at once. Her dog Paddy rested his head on her good leg. Paddy was a Scots Collie she'd raised from a pup, and he had cried every night she was away.

Before she went to bed that Friday night, Tessie let all the girls have a turn at brushing her hair. It was pure white and hung down past her waist. In the firelight it shone like silver, and she did look like a queen being waited on. While we brushed her hair, Tessie petted the pregnant mothercat that had crawled onto her lap right beside Paddy's nose. Mom helped Tessie get good and warm with blankets and a hot water bottle and made sure she took her medicine. "You're good to me, Mary," Tessie would say, and Mom would beam.

Between our father and the boys, they got Tessie up and into her bed in the room off the parlour. Paddy slept under the bed as usual, and a few hours later the mothercat had kittens at the foot of the bed. Tessie refused to let anyone disturb them.

In the morning we awoke to total chaos. Tessie was throwing up and running a fever, Mom was trying to keep her from choking, our father was on the phone trying to get through to the ambulance, and Paddy was barking his head off. We youngest were chased outside with Paddy. We trembled at seeing Tessie leave our house that day, her hair matted and wet, her face pale. We knew she was in pain. Paddy was growling and snarling, and it took three of us to hold him down while the attendants got her in the ambulance. Our parents followed in the car.

Uncertainty and fear hung in the air at home. We didn't know what to do with it. Nervous energy led to tussles among us as the morning passed with no phone call and no "Thanks be to God" from anyone. Getting ready for Hallowe'en was a good distraction for us younger ones. By the time we got our costumes together, we had a little distance from the crisis of the morning. Mom's friend Teresa came over to cook supper for us and stay with our baby brother.

It was a dark, moonless, windy night with just enough rain to make it perfectly spooky. We walked for hours with our neighbour friends and had quite a haul of treats from all the houses we visited. We were just crossing the line fence next to our place when we heard Paddy howling like we'd never heard before. Without saying a word, we all seemed to know we had to go home. We joined hands and ran. Teresa met us at the door, and we knew without being told that Tessie had died. Our exhausted parents came home to a house full of children and an emptiness none of us could comprehend. All went to bed. Few slept. That night, Paddy disappeared, and we never found his bones, though we looked for years afterward.

Tessie was waked in the parlour where so much music and laughter had lightened our hearts. It was a comfort to have so many family and friends around. Though Mom was vulnerable, she was very gracious through the three-day exposure of our home. Neighbours sat up with Tessie both nights while our family went to bed. In the dark, with sleep not coming, our minds wandered. Some of us younger children wondered if the neighbours were there to keep the fairies from getting in or to keep Tessie from getting out.

We grandchildren sat together at the funeral behind Tessie's five children and their spouses. Though it was our first experience as mourners, we held up well. In the weeks after everything was over, our father and Mom were very quiet. They moved downstairs to Tessie's bedroom, and long after our father had gone to sleep, we could often hear Mom crying. She grieved Tessie as she had her own mother.

It was from watching Mom and Tessie that we learned to get along as well as we did, to fight one another one minute and defend one another the next. Otherwise, we'd be suffering strangers.

Paddy Last

I was late, quite late, for my own birth date—
Seven false alarms, so my mother states—
Labour's bad enough, but I made it more intense:
I came out arse-backwards, and I'm like that ever since.
—Yes, I was late.

It was St. Patrick's Day and my middle name's Patricia—
Otherwise I would be named Stephanie Cyrilla.
If you were in my place and you knew that was your fate, Would you
not put your foot down, wouldn't you procastinate?
—That's why I'm late.

I confess that tardiness is something of a habit.
If life were a fairy tale, I'd be Alice's White Rabbit.
Every day is loaded with adventure and distractions,
But when I hear the call I always get there for the action
—But maybe late.

One snowy Boxing Day, with icy roads a factor,
My car lost control, and I collided with a tractor.
It wasn't due to skill—it must have been God's will—
that if we'd hit a second earlier, we'd have all been killed
—But I was late.

I'd love to put it off, but some day I'm gonna die,
And a fancy station wagon's gonna take me for a ride.
When they roll me up the aisle, steeple bells will loudly chime
That the late Margie Carmichael is finally on time.

Olivia

*F*or all there was a war on, it was an exciting time. Young men from all parts of Prince Edward Island left Charlottetown by the boatload, trainload, or planeload, answering the call to join their Commonwealth cousins in combat against the Axis powers devouring Europe.

By the spring of 1940, there were few young men to talk to, dance with, or walk with. The boys too young—or too bad at lying about their age—bided their time on the farms, in the boats, at the factories, or within ear's reach of the nearest radio. Women worked at jobs the men were doing before they went overseas, trained to go overseas themselves, or kept the homefires burning and minded the babies until their dads came home.

For single women the pickings were slim, so when a frigate full of British Navy sailors dropped anchor in Charlottetown for three days in that summer of 1940, it was quite the event. There were tours of the city, banquets for the officers at Fanningbank, and dances in the old hotel and the church halls. For the most part, the married men and women whose wives or husbands were at home or abroad—and the single ones as well—found temptation was secondary to the joy of the dance. Still, chaperones had their work cut out for them, and more than a few pairs of legs slipped through the crowds and out the door.

Olivia O'Neill's legs took her away from her Brighton home to a park bench on lower Prince Street. Beside her, Ensign Albert Mc-Swain from the Northern Irish town of Sligo was stretching out his legs while they watched the moonlight on the quiet water. It was mostly innocent enough, hand-holding, awkward words, two shy people trying to squeeze a lifetime into three brief days, neither understanding the urgency that tugged at them.

Olivia was twenty-one, in training for the nursing corps. The only child of Barrister Kennedy O'Neill and wife Maureen, she was well-acquainted with rules, laws, and judgment. She'd never taken a young man home to meet her parents, for none would have measured up to their expectations for her. Her father was well-respected

but not well-liked, and Olivia was somewhat isolated because of his reputation for arrogance. Her mother was more servant than wife, despite her finery and status. Olivia knew from an early age that theirs was a loveless marriage.

When the frigate sailed, and her sailor with it, she stayed in bed for two days and cried her heart out, telling her mother it was the curse. Six months later, it was obvious that she hadn't had the curse for some time. Her mother took to her bed, and it was her turn to cry for days. Her father was furious and demanded to know who the father was. When Olivia told him, he put his fist through the kitchen window.

"Find out where he is. They'll have to get married as soon as possible," said her mother.

It was the wall that felt the fist next. "It's bad enough she's having a bastard—she'll not marry a goddamn Protestant!"

Olivia left the house and walked for hours. When she returned, her mother was waiting for her. "You'll have to give it up. The sisters will find it a good home, and we can put this all behind us." Olivia wrote a letter to Albert, but none came in reply.

When her son was born, Olivia had no intention of giving him up and would not sign the papers that were sitting on her pillow every time she woke up. In spite of her father, she named her son Brian McSwain. Her father refused to even look at the child. When she was able, Olivia left her home in Brighton and went to live with her cousin, Catherine Coady, on a small farm in the country.

Catherine's husband Peter was a self-taught mechanic who was recruited for training in transport and tank repair. He'd been gone for two years now, and though she had his letters, Catherine had no idea exactly where in Europe he was. They had a five-year-old boy and three-and-a-half-year-old twin girls. Catherine was kind to Olivia and loved young Brian like one of her own. He was a healthy, happy child and Olivia was a devoted mother. The two women became friends, as did their children. For the next four years they coped with responsibility, rationing, and uncertainty, but they kept the home and farm together, sometimes at odds with one another, but at the end of the day they'd say their prayers with the children and Catherine would write her letters to Peter. Olivia wrote no more.

Catherine respected Olivia's privacy and left it up to her if she wanted to tell her about Brian's father, yet the time was coming when Brian would start asking more than "When's daddy coming home?" like her own did. Catherine broached the subject abruptly one evening when they were milking the two cows. They'd already had a tiff that day, so the conversation was terse.

"What are you going to tell Brian when his father doesn't come home?"

"That he's missing in action."

"And have him wait for him the rest of his life? It's not fair to the child."

"What should I tell him, then? That his father dropped anchor in his mother and jumped ship?"

"Tell him the truth, for God's sake—you don't want him hearing it from someone else. You know what it's like here."

"You're damn right I do! Stares and whispers, especially at church, of all places! I'm not the only woman around here that had a child out of wedlock."

"I'm only saying that you should think about telling him soon, that's all."

"I intend to. When I figure out how."

The silence ended with a screech when Catherine's well-aimed squirt from her cow's teat landed right on the face of Olivia, who missed on her first retaliatory shot but landed her second on Catherine's neck, and hit her with a third while Catherine was trying to stop the milk from streaming down her breasts. Before long both women were soaked, but the cows were milked and contented. The women were in better humour, too.

Catherine put fresh straw around the cows. "We're quite the sharpshooters."

"I can see us at the front, blinding the enemy into surrender."

"Twisting Rosie's tail and pulling it back—fire one!"

"Goose-egg grenades!"

"The rusty bucket grenadiers!"

"The jerries would shit themselves."

"So would our husbands." Silence. "I'm sorry, I didn't mean . . ."

"I know."

They took their time walking to the house, with a full bucket of milk between them and a half-bucket each in the other hand. Catherine was looking up at the starry sky.

"What was Albert like? I mean, what caught your eye?"

"My ear actually. It was the Irish accent. 'Would ye be havin' a dance with me?' he says. I was smitten immediately. Didn't hurt that he was handsome, either. What drew you to Peter?"

"It sure as hell wasn't his accent, I'll tell you that. Too North Shore for me. Really, it was his kindness. I was jilted by one of his friends, and he came by a lot to see how I was doing. We were friends first, and I soaked his shoulder good. Then I looked at him one day and realized how much better a man he was than most of them. Two years later we got married."

"From what I've seen of him, he's a gentle soul who loves you and your children. He'll be back, Catherine."

"God willing. Don't you dare give up on happiness, Olivia. You're young and smart and deserve another crack at having a family."

"I'm in no rush. Brian's my family now. I can't thank you enough for giving us a home."

"You and Brian—I don't know what I'd have done if I had to live another winter alone with the three kids. I need you as much as you need me, remember that."

Brian was a few months past his fourth birthday when Olivia's mother finally broke the silence and wrote to her, asking her to bring young Brian in to see her. She was told to come after dinner when her father was at work, and to use the back door. It was a summer afternoon when Brian met his grandmother. She was very cautious at first, but Brian was well-mannered and likable. He wanted to see the garden and play on the swing, but a lame excuse from his grandmother was the signal to Olivia that it was time to go. Her mother didn't want her neighbours to see him just yet.

The awkward gaps in conversation grew shorter with each visit, and Olivia took Brian in once a month when she could get a ride into town. He couldn't wait to meet his grandfather, who was always away when Brian asked about him.

The only reference to Albert McSwain came with each visit.

"What are you going to tell that child?" her mother asked each time.

"I don't know."

Life changed again when the war ended and the troops came home. Catherine's Peter was in the first group that arrived, and the homecoming was storybook. He was one of the lucky ones whose guardian angel took him home whole. There were scars from bullets and shrapnel, but none that would torment his body or mind in the years to come.

As Olivia watched the victory parade in Charlottetown, she was caught up in the excitement like Catherine, the children, and everyone else, until she saw the uniformed nurses marching. She couldn't stop crying when she saw the life she'd wanted walk past and away from her. Brian tugged at her hand. The moment Olivia was dreading came then, swift and sudden. His eyes were dark pools on the edge of overflowing. "My daddy didn't come back." She knelt then, to face those eyes. She shook her head, picked up her son, and walked away from the crowd. Silent tears fell on the shoulders of mother and child. There were no questions, and that evening when Brian said his prayers with his mother, his daddy's name was not on the list.

Six months passed, and Catherine was pregnant again. Things were going well for Peter. His training during the war led to more work than he could find time for. Gradually, whatever livestock they didn't need for their own family was sold off and the fields leased in trade for a portion of the crop. By the time their son John was born, they had a telephone and were planning on getting the electricity in the next year.

It was good for everyone to have a baby in the house, and Peter spent what little spare time he had with the children. He, too, treated Brian like one of his own. Catherine lost a baby early in the next pregnancy, but was pregnant again shortly after. Stephen was born in April of 1947, the same day as Ella Wilson died from pneumonia.

Olivia knew the time was near for leaving but did not know where to go. Though her mother now addressed Brian as her grandson, nothing had changed between Olivia and her father. Catherine and Peter assured Olivia that their home was her home, but that summer when an opportunity came to move, she took it.

The elderly Joseph Wilson was looking for a housekeeper. He and his Ella had had no children, so he was alone, except for his sister next door. He was very fit for his age and planned on farming till the day he died. His home was only a mile down the road from Catherine and Peter. Olivia agreed to keep house in exchange for room and board. Brian was upset with the change, but once he got used to having his own room, he settled in very well—though he still spent most of his days with Catherine and Peter's children.

Mr. Wilson was a quiet, kind man and enjoyed having a young lad around. He treated Olivia with more respect than her father ever gave her mother. He also treated her like a lady and never imposed on her privacy. Every Sunday Olivia and Brian spent with Catherine and her family, and every now and then another guest would be there, some acquaintance of Peter. There was a match-making conspiracy afoot, but Olivia never bit. She was afraid to take a chance, for one thing. For another, very few men would settle for used goods.

The only drawback to her job was Mr. Wilson's sister Jean, a spinster with no sense of humour whatsoever. Worse still, she would also be Brian's teacher when he started school that September. After Olivia and Brian moved in, she made it very clear that she didn't approve of the living arrangement. When she did visit her brother, it was often after supper, usually unannounced, and always an ordeal, for Mr. Wilson would leave the house shortly after his sister arrived, leaving Olivia to sit through the visit.

If Jean wasn't spreading dirt, she was looking for it. Olivia didn't like the woman at all, but knew she had to put up with her. Brian was hearing things he shouldn't hear, and she wondered what Jean said about her behind her back. She shared her frustration with Catherine, who suggested Olivia send Brian over to her house when Jean came, and Catherine would come to visit, too. Catherine's presence eased things, and once Jean was out the door, Olivia and Catherine would either swear or laugh, depending on the nature of the conversation.

One evening after biting their tongues for an hour with Jean, Catherine, just for badness, had some fun with Olivia. "She's terrified you'll marry her brother, you know."

"He's old enough to be my father."

"And you're young enough for more babies."

"Don't be so foolish!"

"And she'd lose her inheritance."

"What?"

"She thinks he's loaded, stashed money all over the house."

"She's crazy as the crows!"

"And just as greedy, but nobody pays attention to her."

"It's a bit sad, isn't it?"

"Don't tell me you have a soft spot for that one."

"No, but she's fairly alone in the world. As much as I complain about her, we are a bit alike in that way."

"You're not like her at all."

"I know, and I have Brian. Maybe if she'd had a child . . ."

"She'd have eaten it!" Catherine collapsed against Olivia in her laughter.

Brian took to school like a duck to water and held his own in the classroom and on the playground. It was a small one-room school next to the church, so he was familiar with most of the thirty-two pupils from grades one to ten. Olivia walked the half-mile to school with Brian for the first week, until she got a note from Miss Wilson telling her that such coddling spoils a child, and it would not be tolerated. Once Brian was in school, Jean's visits got farther apart, which suited Olivia just fine.

Miss Jean Wilson ran the school like a barracks, but it seemed to work, for most of her senior students did very well and many went on to college. Brian excelled in school, though there were several incidents over the first few years when he was roughed up by the older boys. As he got older, more than a few times the word "bastard" was thrown in his face. His mother absorbed the brunt of his anger.

"Why did you lie and pretend you were married?"

"I didn't say I was."

"Then why do I have his name?"

"I had nothing of his to give you but his name."

"I hope he's dead."

The teenage years were rough on both of them. Brian's marks slid as he spent more time carousing with the young fellows than he did helping out at home. What bothered Olivia most was Brian's skipping off on chores Mr. Wilson needed help with. In the tenth grade, everything came to a head. Brian quit school just before Christmas holidays. Olivia couldn't do a thing with him. The air was tense with silent anger, neither mother nor son talking to the other more than was necessary to function, and all of this discomfort was unfair to Mr. Wilson.

When Jean Wilson barged in the door the Friday before school was to resume, Olivia expected she and Brian would get their walking papers. Jean was raging.

"Both of you, sit down and shut up—and don't interrupt me, either. I'm sick and tired of the goings-on between you in this house. Why my brother tolerates it I don't know.

"You—Brian—are a spoiled little arse that needs a swift kick. You're not the only one that never had a father to give it. Ask any of the war widows, they'll tell you! You've seen the half-men that came back, minds gone, drooling all over the place, and the miserable drunks that took the war home with them. Would you trade places with any of their children?

"As for you, Olivia, it's high time you stopped feeling sorry for yourself. Be grateful you have your son and that he's here—and by your choice, not because somebody molested you. Keep on going, hate me all you like, but see to it that Brian's back in school Monday morning."

Neither liked what Jean had to say, but, on Monday, Brian was back in school. Olivia had to admit that as meddlesome as Jean Wilson was, she knew her son and kicked his arse pretty good.

Late in March, Olivia's father telephoned her for the first time, inviting her and the boy for Easter Sunday dinner. Most of her wanted to tell him to go straight to hell, but she told him she would have to discuss it with Brian. Curiosity got the best of her son, and he agreed. Her father hired a driver to pick them up.

It was more an interview than a family gathering, but it was a start. Olivia and her mother were on edge, but Brian set his resentment and nervousness aside and was courteous. His grandfather struggled to make conversation, asking safe questions about Mr. Wilson, sports interests, school, and plans for the future. Brian surprised Olivia when he announced his intention to study medicine. His grandfather was impressed, and Nanna smiled for a change.

Once they were driven home, they were free to speak.

"Mum, I think he's sorry about what he did."

"Brian, you surprise me. I was expecting a tirade. I thought you hated him."

"I don't hate him—but I don't like him either."

"That's understandable."

Brian was silent a few moments. "He's there sometimes, when we visit Nanna."

"How do you know? I've never seen him."

"You weren't looking. I was. Always."

"Did he talk to you?"

"No, he just looked at me, and watched me."

"Why didn't you tell me?"

"I don't know."

"Did it bother you?"

"No. I looked at him, too. Then he'd go."

Over the next few months, when Olivia and Brian saw him again, Olivia's father spent most of the time with Brian, not Olivia, taking him through the house, telling him who was who in the photographs, and walking round the corner for ice cream. Brian didn't share his conversations with Olivia. Though this bothered her, she was mindful that Brian now referred to him as Grandpa.

In July 1956, Kennedy O'Neill died suddenly of heart failure. At his wake, Olivia and Brian stood beside the widowed Maureen and together grieved all that was lost. A week after the funeral, Olivia and Brian moved into the Brighton home.

It was a warm August day, and Brian was watching a baseball game in Victoria Park. Olivia and her mother were sipping lemonade on the screened porch. "Your father was a hard man to understand. It was not an easy life for either of us, and especially for you." From her pocket Maureen took a letter.

"This came six months ago. Your father wouldn't let me tell you. To my knowledge it has not been opened. But in all these years this was the only letter that ever came, I swear to God in heaven."

Olivia took the letter and was trembling so much she could barely make out the postmark. Sligo, Northern Ireland, UK.

Maureen went inside, and Olivia opened the letter.

Dear Miss O'Neill:

My name is Teresa McSwain, mother to Albert. It has taken many years for me to be able to write this letter, and it is still difficult. There is no easy way to tell you but to tell you. My son Albert was killed in action off the coast of France. He was

*one of twenty-five seamen killed by a German bomber. One of
his shipmates accompanied his body home and gave me his personal effects.*

*Among them was your letter. According to his shipmate,
he received it a week before he was killed, and at first he was
quite shocked that he was to be a father, but he was excited once
he got used to it. I don't know if he got to write you back.*

*I was widowed young. Albert was my only child. The
loss is unbearable. I don't know if you made it through the birth,
or kept the child, or if you married someone else, but Albert
was all I loved in this insane world. If he has a son or a daughter,
please tell me where his child is—my grandchild, all I have left
of my son.*

*I'm sorry it has taken so long to write you, and I hope
you have someone to comfort you after reading this. Please
write me back when you're able. I live to hear from you.*

Sincerely,

Mrs. Teresa McSwain

That night, Olivia shared the letter with her son. Brian held his
mother tenderly and together they grieved.

The lonely soul seeks silence in the wee small hours, to be still,
to wrap surrounding shadow like a blanket and wait for dawn to
come and permit rest. After hours of anguish, doubt, and, finally, re-
lease, Olivia lay awake. The moon had set and the birds were stirring.
She got up to make a cup of tea. Going downstairs, she saw light in
the kitchen. She found Brian asleep at the table, head resting on his
hands, a letter under one elbow. She carefully removed it and read:

Dear Mrs. McSwain:

*Thank you for the gift you have given my mother, Olivia
O'Neill, with your letter. My name is Brian McSwain, and your
son Albert was my father. Your letter arrived six months ago,
shortly before my grandfather passed away. It was recently discovered among his papers.*

*Thanks to you, my father is finally real to me. My moth-
er gave me his name and told me as much about him as she knew
of him, but I have so many questions and want to know so much
more about him. I hope in time you can tell me about him.*

I am fifteen years old, a good student and athlete, and

I intend to become a doctor. My mother and I live in my grand-mother's house in the city of Charlottetown. Until this summer, I grew up in a farming community with my mother, my mother's cousins, and many friends and neighbours. Many of the Irish people who settled here say that Ireland and Prince Edward Island are similar. We'll have to visit each other to see how true this is.

My mother raised me herself, and, if I may be bold, she did well. She says I look like my father. I wish I had a photograph to send you. My mother is beautiful and kind. She never married, and I haven't ever heard her speak of wanting to do so. She did not know what had become of your son until she read your letter. I think your news of him is just starting to sink in. She will write to you soon.

We want to meet you, if you want that, too. My other grandmother Maureen says you would be welcome here. I would like to get to know you.

I'm sorry you lost your son and your husband. I'm glad you found us.

Your grandson,
Brian McSwain

Brian stirred as Olivia slipped the letter back under his elbow. She held her breath, and when he settled into sleep again, she tip-toed out of the kitchen. The morning sun shone on the dew, and Olivia's heart began its mending.

She

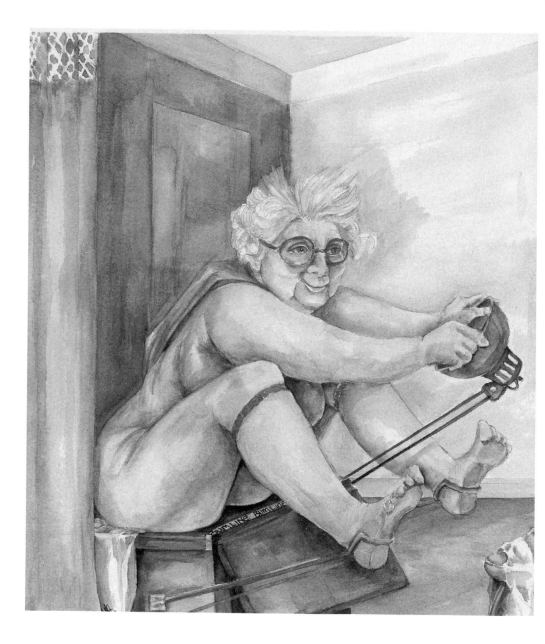

Dear husband, read this note from me and try to understand—
After forty years of marriage, I've done all that I can
To tell you what it feels like when I have an ache or pain
Because you always faint when any body part I name.

Since you are a mechanic and you call your car a "she,"
Perhaps I'll use the good old girl to explain what's wrong with me.
The annual inspection with my doctor was today,
So park yourself in neutral, this is what he had to say.

"Your engine's running fine, all four cylinders full throttle.
You did well on the pressure test, for such an older model.
I'm concerned though for your chassis, it suffers overload.
If you don't lose fifty pounds, a gasket will explode.

"You're really going downhill—you must put on the brakes
To keep from overheating, or else you'll get the shakes.
Your rear end needs alignment, your struts are looking used,
Your disks are wearing down, and I'd recommend new shoes."

That was not the worst of it; he put me on the hoist,
Had my bottom undercoated, and I started making noise—
Rumbling and backfiring, no cruise control at all.
He looked inside and said, "Madam, you need an overhaul!

"You're leaking very badly and burning too much gas.
Your hoses are all clogged and nothing can get past.
If I put a whole new floor in, you'll last for many years,
But today I have to put 'Rejected' on you, dear."

So don't try to turn me over, let me idle for a while.
Like the old girl in the driveway, I'm putting on the miles.
If I'm running cold tonight, don't whine or feel dejected.
I'm just not in the mood for being fuel-injected.

Flora Hill

The Dance

I was seventeen when I met my Willie
We were young and green, my Willie-o and me
My father always wanted me
To marry outside of the family
It can be humiliatin'
When the fella you've been datin'
Is related to you
Darlin', didn't you know?

That's one of the few problems with living in a small rural community in Prince Edward Island: finding a mate. In the late 1950s when I was a young girl growing up in Pleasant Valley, the prospects were scarce. It seemed that all of the nice, friendly, handsome lads were either married, destined for the priesthood, or too closely related. I was pretty well giving up on the whole business, until one summer evening my mother had a good idea.

Mother and I were doing the supper dishes. My older brother Jim was reading the *Patriot*, and Father had CFCY on the radio. We'd just finished listening to the deaths, and since we didn't have a wake to go to, we were having a quiet evening at home.

"Listen to this, Flora," says Jim. "Old Dooley's looking for a housekeeper again." Dooley was our neighbour down the road, a contrary eighty-five-year-old bachelor always looking for a housekeeper when what he really wanted was a wife. But no woman or girl would work for him long because he was what my mother called an "old ram." "You'll be marrying him yet, Flora," says Jim.

"No, she won't!" says Mother.

"He's related," says Father.

The announcements came on and Mother says, "Did you hear that, Flora? There's a dance Friday night at the Tignish Legion. You and Jim should go."

"Mother," says Jim. "I've heard stories about Tignish that would curl your hair. Too wild for Flora."

"Now, Jim," says Father, "everybody knows that the fine people of Tignish make up those stories themselves to keep the riff-raff away."

"The bloodlines around here are getting pretty thin," says Mother, "and if Flora's ever going to get out and see the world, she may as well start with Tignish. Jim, you're taking her."

So, two nights later, off we went, all the way to Tignish. Jim wasn't too pleased with having me along, but after he visited a few bootleggers on the way, he was in better humour. There was quite a crowd gathering by the time we got to the Tignish Legion, and Jim and I didn't know a soul. I was nervous, but I was excited, too.

When we walked in the door, I thought I was on another planet. The people had such different features from the ones down home— short and sturdy frames, darker hair, smaller noses, bigger ears, more hair on the ears—and they got right quiet when we came in. Even the band stopped playing. I thought it was very respectful and welcoming. Jim didn't think so, and he went back out to the car for a snort. Once the band got going again, the mosquitoes were terrible, but the band was worse.

At the local dances I usually hid in the back corner. The girls called me "Wall-Flora." That night, though, for some strange reason I felt like a new girl, and I acted like one. I sat right in the centre of the row of chairs along the left wall. The girls were seated all around the perimeter, and the lads paraded past us like geese. There was a standard protocol in place at most dances: if a girl didn't dance with the first lad that asked her, none of the rest would ask her up all night.

Imagine my surprise when a good-looking lad with all his teeth held his hand out to me and lisped ever so sweetly, "Will you dance?" I had no time to say yes, for he hauled me up and onto the dance floor. Well! What a dance we had. He had two left feet and I had two right, so once we got our bearings, we never left the floor. His name was Willie Hill, and right away we got into the Island interview to see if we were related. We shared the family names starting at the As and were successfully working our way through the Ps when the brawl broke out.

It was a continuation of the brawl from the week before. The strapping Summerside lads were back for more from the locals. It started in the right corner by the door. When they started taking off their shirts, I got all warm and dizzy. The tans on them! From waist to forehead. I couldn't believe it. Once they got going at it, the dustbane was useless and after only a minute it was hard to see who was fighting who. It was like watching a dust storm, moving to the centre and getting bigger as more were pulled into the fray. Jim got into it, and Willie was yanked in right after him.

It got worse after the girls joined in. They hauled the chairs from the wall and closed the lads in. Some of the girls got up on the chairs, took their high-heels off, and started hitting each other's lads on their heads. Then they went at each other, pulling hair, biting, and scratching. God help the ones that had sunburns! I was so scared I went and hid behind the toilet door, but I still had a good view.

Suddenly there was a roar from the door and in storms Father Flynn, who wasn't too pleased to be roused out of bed by the shenanigans across the road. He was a huge man, and he was fuming! With two Hail Marys and not much grace, in ten minutes flat he cleared out the Legion faster than a call-to-arms. I came out of hiding when I thought it was safe. The place was a mess, broken chairs and tables, shirts that smelled like blood, booze, and sweat, and shoes everywhere. No sign of Jim. I was all alone in the Tignish Legion.

Then I heard a low moan coming from under one of the broken tables. "Oh me head... oh me tooph... where's me eyes..."

I lifted up the tabletop, and there was Willie, with two black eyes, a good-sized goose-egg on his forehead, and one of his beautiful teeth missing. When he saw me, he grinned from ear to ear and said, "Wanna do this again next week?"

"Oh yes!" says I.

Just then Jim came in to take me home. He wasn't much worse for wear, not anything like Willie was. Just before I went out the door, Willie yelled, "Don't forget your high-heels!" We were as good as engaged.

Jim was all talk on the way home, about the brawl, and the swearing of "Fightin' Father Flynn," as he was called by the whole Western end of the Island. "Yeah, that Flynn is a credit to the priesthood," he said. "The lad I was fighting with took me out to his car after and gave me the nicest drink of shine I ever had... good, hard-working moss-gatherer, really friendly. I'd fight him again."

"There's another dance there next week," I told him. Jim looked at me and smiled. "Our little Flora's growing up."

I smiled back, "The girls will be calling me 'Wild-Flora' after next week!"

Vocation

I kissed my first corpse when I was five years old. Her name was Angelina. I'll never forget it. It was like kissing an old turnip after the frost got into it. I met Angelina only a few times before, and she reminded me of the big Raggedy Ann doll I saw in the Eaton's store window. She was a happy old woman with a broad, thin-lipped smile. She flitted around her kitchen, all arms and legs, and there was a scent of Jergen's lotion in the air as she passed. In the casket, though, she didn't look like herself at all.

Her face was spread out all over the pillow like a full moon, and her smile was gone, making her look unhappy. Her skin was covered in some paste that smelled worse than old sweat on a dirty dog. Between that and the musty flowers, I gagged and nearly threw up on her. Mother was mortified. "That's the last time I'm taking you to a wake!" she said, and dragged me out of there. I didn't even get to shake hands with anybody or have any lunch. I was very disappointed.

Some would call such an experience traumatic, but for me it was more a calling, and I begged Mother to give me another chance. She relented eventually, and by the time I was seven I was as good at the sorry-for-your-troubles as any grown-up. I was fascinated with how the corpses looked, and a lot of the time I wasn't too impressed with the bodywork. I thought, "God, I could do better than that!" and the seeds were planted for what turned out to be a vocation of sorts: to make the dead look their best at their worst.

I practised on the turnips with my mother's cosmetics, and I'd probably make a fortune off the tourists with those creations today. The horses were very patient with me braiding their tails and experimenting with different styles and cuts on their manes. Father was very supportive and encouraged me a lot. Mother wasn't too pleased with running out of rouge and hairspray all the time, but Father said, "Leave her be, dear. It'll pay off someday." How right he was, though it was many years before it happened, and he didn't live to see it.

I finished grade ten and got married shortly after, farming with my husband Willie and raising two boys. I cut their hair and got a lot of honourable mentions for animal grooming at the local fairs. Willie died young, and I waited home till our boys were grown and on their own. Then I went back to school, taking a course in Cosmetology, specializing in hair, make-up, nails, and wardrobe.

Though I'd been aspiring to it all those years, I never did up a real corpse till my Aunt Gloria died. She was a bright spark, that one, enjoyed every minute of her life and prided herself on her appearance. So when she knew she was going to die, she asked me if I'd do her up. I was honoured, of course, and not long after, I headed into the funeral home in Charlottetown to prepare her body for burial.

I arrived early to find a lady from the Sally Anne Beauty Room slapping on the paint while the perm was setting in Aunt Gloria's hair. I took the sponge out of her hand. "Scrape that off right now," I told her. "Gloria wouldn't be caught dead with all that guck on!"

She gave me a hateful look. "This is my corpse," she said, "Mr. Coffin's paying me to do this one—go find your own corpse, why don't you?"

The nerve of some people! I tried being polite and professional. "She's my Aunt Gloria, and I'll thank you to take your curlers and leave us alone," I said.

"Like hell I will," she says, and chased me around the table, with poor old Gloria lying there on the steel table, stark naked but for the curlers in her hair.

Next thing you know, the other one banged into the table and Gloria went flying and landed face-down on the floor and broke her nose! The other one let out a screech to wake the dead, but Gloria never budged. I was furious. "Haven't you done enough already? Do you have to burst her eardrums too? Get out of here right now!" She slipped on one of the curlers that fell out of Gloria's hair, and I almost had another corpse to do up. I was some glad to see the back of that one.

What a time I had getting Gloria back on the table. She was never too flexible at the best of times, and that day was no different. I did the best I could with her nose, and I must've done pretty good because there were more than a few at the wake who thought she must've had a nose job and wondered which plastic surgeon she went to. The red taffeta dress looked elegant, a centrepiece that set off the white lining and the dark walnut wood of her casket. Her hands caressed a silver-coloured rosary, laced through the stubby farm fingers that were as delicate as fine china. I left the garden soil under the nail of the thumb that was covered up by the rosary, just so she could take a little piece of the Island with her.

To give credit where it's due, though, the Sally Anne perm really suited her. Her hair made her look just like a corpse should look—

dead. It was a labour of love to do her up, though, and, in the end, I had Gloria looking better than she had in a long time.

The word got around, and soon I was doing up corpses once or twice a week until I retired a few years ago. Over the years I've done up quite a few friends, and relatives too, and though it's hard, there's reward in being entrusted with safe-guarding precious human dignity. These days I'm mainly on call for the funeral co-ops, volunteering wherever I'm needed.

If I had one wish—though some might call it fantasy—I'd like to live long enough to do up Leonard Cohen when he dies—if he dies. I've always had a thing for him and his depressing music. He reminds me of an old roaming black Labrador retriever we had on the farm and had to put down because he was old and tired from years of breeding.

I can picture Leonard in his new-age crystal casket, his song "The Singer Must Die" playing in the background, the fleeting smile captured on his five-o'clock-shadow face, and him lying on cream-coloured silk, naked from the waist down. I'm not attracted to him—though if I was, in my day I'd have given any one of those wispy women of his a run for their money.

Given a crack at Leonard, I could do him up so that even as a dead man he could still tempt the angels and make any of us mortals swoon, from the hardest old widow to the youngest young pup.

Eulogy

In the funeral business, there's all sorts of surprises, just like in the *Guardian* sometimes. Some of the errors are funny enough, but the corrections are hilarious. I saw this notice on the back page a few months ago and thought it was a prank:

> NOTICE OF TENDER
> To compose Eulogy for recently deceased.
> Creative Writing Course an asset.
> Lowest Tender not necessarily accepted.
> Apply to File 37172 in care of this newspaper.

It wasn't a prank after all, and two days later the notice appeared in bigger print. I thought it must be some bigwig looking for a prestigious send-off. I was intrigued, so I put in a tender—and didn't I get it! Most of the others withdrew their tenders once they found out who it was—a man named Alfred. I didn't know the man from a hole in the wall, but I thought the eulogy-writing practice would be good for writing my memoirs someday.

So off I went to Tim Horton's to meet Alfred's mourners—all four of them: Alfred's parents, aunt, and uncle. They were an unusually cheery family given the circumstances, but, as we got to talking, I began to understand. Alfred's parents had been away from the Island and hadn't seen the aunt and uncle—or each other—for many years, so it was a bit of a reunion, which isn't unusual when it comes to wakes and funerals, at least here on the Island.

What was unusual, though, was the family's dilemma. The nature of Alfred's case warranted a closed-casket wake, but Alfred's parents insisted on an open casket so that they could see their little boy one more time and make sure he was really dead. They told me there weren't any takers when they shopped around for a funeral home. Alfred's reputation preceded him, and the funeral directors were leery of a lawsuit. On the family's behalf, I made a call from Tim's to one of the more "co-operative" funeral homes, and the director consented to having the wake and the chapel service—if I took full responsibility for preparing the body, and if the family signed a waiver.

Once that matter was laid to rest, between Timbits, I heard the pathetic story of Alfred's life. By the time we got to the funeral home that evening, I was excited by the challenge that awaited me. While the family worked out arrangements with the funeral director, I went to the cold room to meet Alfred.

He was in bad shape, but after a chiropractic technique or two he straightened out and relaxed a bit. His father had said he was never "all there," but I found Alfred's missing ear among his personal items. All in all, except for the dent in his skull, he was fairly intact, and I don't doubt for one minute that he might have been handsome as a baby.

I always talk to my clients while I work on them, to let them know what I'm doing and why. A good distraction for all concerned. I found it hard to make conversation with Alfred at first, but once I stapled his ear back on, he was a surprisingly good listener.

As a freelance fix'er-upper, I do most of my work with the smaller funeral homes, though I've been in the others by request. I've always done up people I knew or who were known to me. Alfred was a newbie, so I opened my satchel and showed him all the tools of my trade: scissors, crazy glue, combs and brushes, tweezers, nail clippers, stapler, needles and thread, lotions and powders, razors and shaving cream, cotton balls, scent-free makeup, gels and sprays.

Calamine lotion is a good primer and raises the skin tone. If there's seam-filling needed (especially on lifelong tan fanatics), I'll mix in some baby powder with it. Once dried, it's easy to sand and buff. As for base coat, it varies—the bigger the bruise, the more I use. It's not complicated. I aim for a "natural" look, though in Alfred's case, working with the photo the family had given me, I wasn't sure there was such a thing.

While I worked on his face, I told him about the time I was doing up a retired storekeeper in Summerside and had no glue for his eyelids, so I improvised with denture gum I had in my purse. It worked fine until he was under the pink lamp at the wake. The gum got soft and I saw one eye starting to open, so I went through the line again to discreetly close it. A few minutes later, it was opening up again. And again. I was on my fifth time through the line-up when the widow cried out, "Angus! Stop yer flirtin'!"

I told Alfred about when my elderly neighbour Lila died and her only sister Josie came home from Toronto. Both were spinsters, but different as night and day. Lila was an easygoing, gentle woman, and she let Josie boss her around for years. Josie and I went shopping for Lila at Sears. I spied a beautiful dusty rose dress with a delicate collar and wrist trim that looked like Queen Anne's lace, which Lila's orchard was full of. No sooner had I taken the dress off the rack than Josie grabbed it, tried it on, and bought it for herself! She picked out a drab gabardine suit for Lila. I fixed Josie, though. I went back to Sears later that afternoon and exchanged the suit for the dusty rose dress, in the next size down. It was worth the extra money to see Josie upstaged by Lila.

It helps to have a sense of humour when the job is difficult. Thank God the family provided a toupée for Alfred, for I couldn't have done a thing with his hair even if they could've found it. There was a crater where his crown was missing, but half a bag of cotton balls filled that void, and Alfred finally had his head together.

He may have lacked a lot of things in life, but taste was not one of them. The suit I dressed him in was from his Armani collection, a lightweight dark tweed with white silk shirt and black silk tie.

It's hard to imagine bonding with someone dead, but it happens in my line of work. Dignity is everyone's right, and the body's last touch with the living should be a gentle and loving one. With Alfred, though, I had my work cut out for me and had to make a lot of adjustments in order to get a sense of who he was. Call me foolish, but I had a feeling he was grateful—though that didn't fit the family's profile of him.

There weren't many at the wake, but he sure drew a crowd at the funeral. If didn't hurt that I put out a sandwich board on the front lawn of the funeral home: "Lunch to Follow." Gets Islanders every time!

I read Alfred's eulogy to a full house.

Dear Lord, we are assembled here today to send back to you our brother Alfred. Though his time here was short, we here have deemed it long enough for the likes of that fellow! Where do we begin when we tell of Alfred? Well, where do any of us begin but in the twinkle of somebody's eye?

That's all he was at first, and quite a surprise to his father when he landed on the family farm at the age of three with a note pinned to his jacket: "Dear Frank. Here's our son, Alfred. He's all yours! Good luck. Alice."

It didn't take long to figure out why his mother gave him to Frank. He was a boisterous, energetic little fellow, always doing something naughty—like breaking things, getting into fights, setting fires—but he was a big help when it came time for killing the chickens for the deep-freeze.

He had an awful pick on the Eaton's Santa Claus. Poor Santa hated to see him coming. On the Christmas just before he turned five, Alfred and Santa got off on the wrong foot again. Alfred got mad and pulled Santa's beard off. "See? This isn't Santa!" he yelled at the children and parents waiting in line. "He's an old bum they picked up off Queen Street and sobered up. He's just working off his fine. If he could read, he'd already know what you want for Christmas, don't you think? You wouldn't have to stand here all day pretending you believe either, now would you? This isn't Santa—there is no Santa."

Every child in the store was crying, and the parents were ready to kill him. Alfred was banned from Eaton's till he was twenty-one.

That pretty well finished Frank. He couldn't stand the strain of single parenthood any more, so he ran away from home.

The challenge of raising Alfred fell to his father's sister Aunt Ella and her husband Uncle Earl, who took him into their home. They said it was a labour of love and a test of their faith, and they lost all interest in having any of their own. On the day Alfred left their home for good, they had a priest come in to bless the house.

Now you'd think that someone like Alfred would have ended up in jail or in politics. No sirree! Not Alfred. He put all of his unique talents to work and slithered his way right through law school. God, he was a good lawyer! He defended the scum of the earth and had them looking like angels by the time he got through with the witnesses. His associates said his approach was to take a thumbscrew to the truth. In no time at all he'd have the witnesses recanting testimony and begging for a recess. Some of them would get charged with perjury, and Alfred would charm or coerce them into hiring him to represent them, and he'd get them off!

Sadly, though, that kind of dedication leaves little room for peace and companionship, and it's said that Alfred spent many a late night alone walking the streets of Charlottetown, one step ahead of his miserable little shadow, looking down at his weary feet as he plodded along.

Perhaps if he had looked up four nights ago, he might have seen the stars or the moon—or the concrete slab that fell on him from the roof of that Richmond Street building. Alfred certainly left a lasting impression.

At the age of thirty-seven, Alfred is gone, and with him go our prayers and hopes for his eternal future. Now he stands in front of the Supreme Court, and as God is my witness, I hope Alfred has a good lawyer. He'll be looking in the "Lower" Courts, that's for sure!

After it was all over, I gave his family a photo I found in the breast pocket of Alfred's suit, and their tears finally came. It was a young smiling Alfred astride a Percheron mare, and a proud father holding the horse's bridle. To this day, I wonder where that child went.

Passage

Today was the turning of an age in my family. A priceless heirloom that had been in our family for generations went to a complete stranger. I couldn't count the number of men, women, and children that enjoyed its woody warmth, wringing their hands in anticipation of using it, and releasing long-awaited sighs of satisfaction from a job well done. Today that tradition ended with me. I gave away the outhouse.

It was originally a one-seater my mother's grandfather made for her grandmother when they got married, and it was always passed on through the daughters. It started out simple enough (a few rough boards and a hole, four sides, a door, and a slanted roof), but the old boy got into the shingling. Then he put in a window with a box of flowers growing on the outside and the inside. It really looked like a house then—a home away from home.

Many's the name that was dreamed up for all the babies while their mothers and fathers sat in there. There was a verandah on it at one time, but after a while a person gets tired of the neighbours stopping by for a chat, so it was taken off when I was a little girl.

That didn't go over too good with the one next door, gossipy old Jenny Miller. She thought we were being uppity wanting to be so private, and for years she never said as much as a how-are-you to any of us. You should have heard her the day we got the running water in. Over she came, sweet as pie all of a sudden, wondering if we'd be wanting to get rid of the old outhouse now that we had the new "throne room," as she called it. She was awfully put out when she was told it was being kept for me, and she never said a word to any of us for a few more years, till the night of my bridal shower.

I was having a wonderful time. All the women from around were playing games with clothespins and flyswatters and enjoying the spread my Aunt Alma put on. I was sitting like the Queen on an armchair decorated with homemade tissue flowers, and everyone thought I looked fairly regal with the pie-plate hat they had tied on my head with ribbons and bows.

My cousin Jean, my maid-of-honour, passed the gifts to me while Aunt Alma read the cards. I was especially touched when Aunt Alma read Jenny Miller's card, since I wasn't sure she'd come. When I opened her gift, I started to cry—it was a beautiful royal blue enamel chamber pot! "Oh, Jenny," says I, "you shouldn't have!"

"Oh well, I should have," says Jenny, "for that Willie Hill you're marryin' doesn't have a pot to piss in."

Everybody held their breath, waiting for me to burst out crying, but I didn't. No. I walked straight over to where Jenny was sitting, took that chamber pot, and put it upside-down on top of her miserable little blue-haired head! "A pity it isn't full," says I and went right back to my bridal chair, sat down, and opened the rest of my presents. Home Jenny went, pot and all.

When I married Willie, we shared the house with his mother and father. The outhouse went with me as part of my dowry, and Willie put it up next to theirs in the hardwood grove behind the house. He took out the connecting sides—and the two became one. Willie built birdhouses all over the grove. We went in there together sometimes just to watch the birds. Willie adored the robins most of all. In the spring of the year he'd run into the kitchen all excited: "Flora! Robin red-breast is back!" Then he'd swing me around the kitchen floor till we were dizzy. We'd often go to the outhouse together just to get some time alone away from his parents. On a quiet summer day we could hear the bees buzzing around the flowers in the window box. Honest to God, I didn't know a thing about the birds or the bees till I married Willie, and he knew a lot for a fellow without much education.

His father and mother died, one behind the other when our two boys were just starting school. We put a bathroom in their bedroom a year later, but we didn't use it all that much for a while, and the outhouse was a great place to get some time away from the boys. Poor little lads, they were barely into their teens when their daddy dropped dead of a sudden heart attack.

After my Willie died, things changed quite a bit. I didn't hear the birds or the bees or the wind in the grove for a long, long time. Everything seemed so empty without him, especially the outhouse, so I stopped using it altogether for years. I didn't have daughters to pass it on to, and neither of my daughters-in-law had any real feeling for it, so it just sat there in the grove. I was even wishing old Jenny Miller was still alive. I would've given it to her.

Just this morning, a hippie fellow that moved here from New Hampshire drove into my yard and asked me if I'd consider selling him the outhouse. I thought of all the shifty, conniving antique dealers that had tried to get it off me over the years, and I was about to say no when he said, "Listen! Is that a robin red-breast I hear?"

I started crying, and I longed so for my Willie. "Go ahead, dear," I says. "You take it."

God love him, he felt so bad. "Are you sure?" he says.

"Yes," says I. "It's time. It'll be in good hands." The wonder in his eyes reminded me of Willie when he'd hold our babies.

"You know," he said, "I always dreamed of having an outhouse, since I was a little boy—but I never wanted to kill a tree just so I could indulge in selfish solitude and contemplation. I'll take good care of it, Mrs. Hill, and you feel free drop in and use it any time you want, you hear?"

He brought some men with him a few hours ago, and they loaded it onto a flatbed trailer. As I watched the outhouse go down the lane and disappear into the dusty summer evening, I could swear I saw Willie, his parents and my parents, our aunts and uncles, sisters and brothers, cousins and neighbours, all sorts of shadowy hands waving goodbye.

Red Dirt Road

Oh, the red dirt road wasn't easy travelling
Especially early in the spring
Mud to the belly made many turn back—
Forget about planning anything
People got their horses out and graded it themselves—
They didn't need a road machine
They didn't need politicians to improve the conditions
And the grass grew green

On the red dirt road

Riding to the ceilidhs, dropping in on the neighbours,
Church on Sunday, too
Never made strangers of the people next door
Like these times tend to do
The doctor came by when anyone was sick
Half the time he never got a cent
Yeah the red dirt road made neighbors of us all
And we were all content

Then the auto was invented, the horses were tormented
Till everybody started giving in
Soon a lot of them were driving fancy little rigs
And they were sporting their expensive little grins
They widened all the ruts, they raised a lot of dust
That settled on the wagon and the sleigh
When the red dirt road wasn't coping with the load
They paved it away

I grew up on a red dirt road
My feet got tough on a red dirt road
I fell in love on a red dirt road

the red dirt road... mud oozes through your toes
the red dirt road... take your sweetie for a stroll
the red dirt road... say hello to Uncle Joe

the red dirt road... clip-clopping of the mare
the red dirt road... hip-hopping of the hare
the red dirt road... I'm wishing I was there

the red dirt road... drip-dropping of the rain
the red dirt road... flip-flopping of the mane
the red dirt road... I'm coming home again

Margie Carmichael is a Prince Edward Island musician, song-writer, playwright, and storyteller whose works have travelled across Canada, the US, and into the UK, through her performances at festivals, on CBC and BBC radio, and on her own music CDs; as well as being performed by other artists. Her play, *Scenes from a Wake*, based on the character Flora Hill, won first prize in the New Voices Playwriting Competition and was performed by Theatre PEI across the Island. Mulgrave Road Theatre later toured a version called *Raining Cats and Daughters* throughout Nova Scotia and PEI. She lives in Pisquid with husband Michael Scotto and sons John and Mark. This is her first book.

Dale McNevin is a Charlottetown artist and book illustrator (*The True Meaning of Crumbfest, Everything That Shines,* and *Three Tall Trees*). This book began as a collaboration with her original painting and Margie's companion poem, which were first published in the Maritime Centre of Excellence for Women's Health 2000 Calendar.